SAM AND SOFIA:

THE MAGIC OF THE STARS

First published by Dog Ear Publishing
8888 Keystone Crossing
Suite 1300
Indianapolis, IN 46240
www.dogearpublishing.net

ISBN: 978-145756-898-5

This book is printed on acid-free paper.
Printed in the United States of America

Dedicated To My Fifth Grade Class

Special Thanks To

Mom, Dad, Sister Taylor

My Editor, Sarah Chase

And Most Of All, My Best Friend, Eleanor
For being my family, my second family,
my inspiration, and supporting me as I wrote this book

By Brady Woodhouse

CHAPTER 1:

ONCE UPON A TIME

Once Upon A Time…

Sam and Sofia, twin sisters, were facing a large dragon, with scales larger than their faces. Their faces looked as if someone had slapped them. They ran away at full pace, but the dragon was too fast. For the first time, they looked to the side and saw their shared room, Sam's bed on the right and Sofia's on the left. They ran across the now wooden floor, not knowing how they would escape the situation. They jumped into their beds, and Sam suddenly woke up in her bed looking into the darkness.

Sam looked down at her hands which were now fiddling with the blankets on her warm bed. She turned over, felt her bed, and realized that she had peed, probably because of her dream.

"Oh darn," Sam said tossing her covers off aggressively. She stood up and just decided to sleep on the couch.

Before she went to sleep, she kept wondering if there was a reason for the dream, like a signal about what would happen in the future.

* * *

"Hey Sam, where are you?" Sam heard the voice as she blinked her eyes open. She sat up and rubbed her eyes until she felt satisfied.

"I'm down here," Sam said as she stood up from the couch. She let out a yawn right after and ran up the stairs to see her sister.

"Are you ready for school," she heard as she walked up the final step and saw her sister.

"Yeah," Sam said as she started to pull out her fingers to count. "It's just kind of nerve-racking how, one we were just in the fourth grade, but we skipped a grade, and two we moved from Minnesota to Florida last week."

"I guess so," Sofia said as she leaned her head down a bit. "But new school, new friends, new house, new state, and best of all, the beach, so don't be worried."

"Okay," Sam said as she walked over to go find the clothes she would wear.

As she searched through her closet she thought about her mom, who had died just a couple of months ago on a business trip. The plane had been going from Minnesota to Italy, but had crashed in France. The pilot had gotten food poisoning and couldn't maneuver the plane. And though the co-pilot should have helped, it was his first time and he was a tad nervous.

But at least Dad had gotten a job in Florida, so they could start over.

Sam put on her clothes in the bathroom on the second level and grabbed her school supplies.

"Are you ready to go?!" Dad asked as he yelled up the stairs.

"Coming!" Sofia said as they put their backpacks on and walked down the stairs. They stepped out of the house and onto the sidewalk, and Dad led them to his car across the suburban streets.

Sam stepped into the car feeling as if she had stepped through a barrier, as though now her life would have a fresh start.

CHAPTER 2:

A SITUATION

"You ready for school, girls?" Dad asked. They saw him looking straight at them through the mirror.

"We could've walked by ourselves," Sofia said looking to her sister, Sam.

"Do you not need me anymore?" Dad said, starting to tear up. "Wah, wah, wah!"

"We know you're not really crying," Sam said, cracking a smile at Dad.

"And by the way, it's only because you're going to be late for work," Sofia said.

"Well it's your first day, I want to be here," Dad replied as he looked back at them with a smirk. He took a right and they saw their school on the left side of the road.

"Here's school," Sofia said. "Love you."

"So, do I," Sam said.

"Me too," Dad said as they got out of the car and stepped on the sidewalk.

Sofia and Sam saw the school. It had a large wooden door with a metal handle, and a lot of students were hanging around the bike racks. There was a sign that said *Taylor's Private Day School. Pre-K—Eighth Grade.* Some of the younger children were hiding in the foliage on the side of the school yard, and some of the older kids were hitting a coconut tree trying to get a coconut to fall.

Sam looked up at the daunting school, and Sofia looked around the yard with all the new faces. Sam said slowly and lightly, "Here we go."

* * *

Sofia and Sam were in the schoolyard at recess. They sat on a bench complaining about how their teachers got so mad when they corrected them. A girl walked up to Sam and Sofia. "Hello. My name is Sabine," the girl said. "What are yours?"

"Sam."

"Sofia."

Sabine had long brown hair, misty blue eyes, and lots of freckles on her nose. "I don't remember you from fifth grade," Sabine said. "You must be new."

"Actually, we skipped fifth grade," Sam said, making a five with her hands.

"We are also from a different state," Sofia added.

"Wait, so you're a year younger?" Sabine clarified as she became less airy and happy.

"What's wrong with that?" Sofia asked as she turned her head a little.

"It's just that there's a guy in our class named Max who is supposedly popular, and he doesn't welcome people who think that education is useful. His group is over there," Sabine said with a snarky voice as she pointed to the monkey bars surrounded by bushes that were wilting from the heat.

"Why would he do that?" Sofia asked looking over at the monkey bars.

"I call him Max the Meanie," Sabine replied. "Last year there was a test to get to the sixth grade. I was the only one who got an A+, and Max got a C. He ripped my test, and I had to do it over again because I needed it next year, and he told me I had to get a B or lower or I wouldn't be included with his group."

"Well, has the teacher talked to this Max?" Sofia asked, concerned.

"Anyone who tells the teacher isn't welcomed," Sabine said.

"We will tell them that we skipped the fifth grade, and we won't care if he doesn't include us," Sofia said as she marched over to the monkey bars next to which the group was following Max by climbing the coconut tree. Sam quickly followed.

"See you later," Sabine walked away from the bench.

Sofia and Sam integrated themselves into the group. They mingled and introduced themselves. They also emphasized that they had skipped a grade. Once Sofia had told the one hanging from the coconut tree, he jumped down and started laughing.

"What," Sofia asked as she looked at him with a stare.

"Funny," Max said as he stood upright again. "Oh. You did skip a grade?"

"Uh huh," Sam said now realizing that Sabine was right.

"Well why?" Max asked. "It's not like education is going to get you anywhere in life."

"Maybe it will," Sofia said standing a little taller.

"Okay," Max said as he held up his hands. He started to talk to other people, telling them to leave. They all left to go sit on the swings.

For the first time, Sam and Sofia noticed many students stood by themselves. These students looked down at their shoes, or wrote in a book, or even just stared straight forward, as if they were ashamed. It was almost like those students were outcasts, all alone. But they outnumbered the number of students in the monkey bars group.

* * *

Sofia and Sam entered the cafeteria at lunch and went over to where some of the outcasts were. Max went up to one, and the unfairly treated outcasts said that they would go and then they got up and left. Sam and Sofia were stuck sitting by the trash can. Sabine was right. The only way to stop this would be in a magical realm of possibility and hope. Nowhere like this unwelcoming, harsh, and just downright mean middle school.

* * *

Sam and Sofia got home and walked directly up to their room frustrated about their day at school. They were on their beds doing their early year homework.

A giant boom sounded from outside.

THOOM! CRASH! "IT ALMOST HIT ME!"

Sam and Sofia bolted downstairs and looked to Dad who was looking at an email on his computer, completely ignoring the crash.

Sam and Sofia looked at him instantly, "You can go," Dad said as he looked back to his computer and continued with his work.

Sam and Sofia were out the door in seconds wandering about the commotion.

CHAPTER 3:

THAT NOISE

Sam and Sofia had never seen so many people crowding the streets of Miami. They couldn't even see the actual street. The place felt like it was vibrating. It was hard to breathe. Everyone was rushing to where they heard the noise.

"What was that noise?" they asked. Or, "It came from over there!" they shouted.

Once the twins got to where the crowd was forming, they started to squeeze through everyone who was tightly jammed together. Sam and Sofia tried to get a good view of the giant black blob, an asteroid that fell from the sky into the park.

When the twins finally got to the front of the packed crowd, they were so close together that it felt like they were hugging each other. Sofia and Sam saw where the asteroid crashed into the earth. Although the crash made a loud sound, the asteroid was surprisingly small, with maybe a volume of only three-cubic feet. They also saw black splotches of space dust powdered onto the earth. Next to the asteroid were deep cracks in the ground.

The twins heard the mayor start to talk. "Don't worry, don't worry. Everything is under control. We will put this asteroid where it belongs, and you won't have to worry," the mayor said. A translator next to him was repeating everything in Spanish.

Sam finally got a good glance at the rock while she peered in between a window of other people's heads. She saw some odd patterns on the rocky surface. But that wasn't everything. While everyone else was watching the mayor speak, she saw a little peak of pinkish light glow from the asteroid.

I must be losing my mind, she thought. But that didn't stop her from wanting the asteroid. She had to admit to herself, she thought the rock looked cool. She stared at it. She knew she needed to have it.

"I'll take the asteroid to my house," Sam blurted out loudly.

"What in the world are you thinking, Sam?" Sofia whispered.

"That it's cool, but I don't think you'd follow along if I told you my thoughts," Sam responded.

"I hope your *thoughts* know what they're doing." Sofia sounded worried.

"We are going to take it back to the labs," the mayor said. When he looked at the asteroid for a few seconds, the pinkish light was shining at him, too. "Are you sure you want it?" the mayor asked robotically, according to Sam. The asteroid seemed to hypnotize him.

"Want it? I adore it! I would fight for it," Sam said. She spoke a little as if it were her child during the last part.

"Little scary, but okay," the mayor said still sounding hypnotized. "And the asteroid is going to this young girl named?" The mayor stopped. "What's your name?"

"Sam," she responded.

"This young girl named Sam!" the mayor announced as he corrected his earlier mistake.

"Yes!" Sam excitedly whispered under her breath.

She tried to pick up the small asteroid in her two hands. But it was heavy, so she rolled the asteroid as she pushed it down the streets toward home. They saw a police car ahead of them and the mayor shooed it off to the side of them in a very structured manner.

* * *

On their walk home, Sam couldn't prevent herself from saying, "Eee!" Sofia and Sam walked down the streets with the skinny lanes for the third time today.

"Hey! I said you could check out the scene," Dad said, with surprise in his voice as he watched the asteroid roll across the floors of the home.

"The mayor gave it to us!" Sam said excitedly.

"Yeah," Sofia said, sweating from the pushing. "It was like he was mesmerized."

"Let me help you take that to your room," Dad said as he wedged his hands under the asteroid and slowly picked it up with help from Sam and Sofia.

After they got up the stairs and in their room, the twins stared at it in awe.

Surprisingly, even though Sofia had said she didn't want it, when she looked at it again, she thought the asteroid was cool because she realized it wasn't dangerous. She also loved the design.

"I thought this would be dangerous, but now it seems cool having a piece of space in your own room," Sofia said.

"I know," Sam said excitedly.

Sam and Sofia both slid their hands over the asteroid until they memorized every piece of texture there was.

"There has to be something more about this asteroid, I mean why is it so small, are there some kind of molecules in here that could make a giant scientific breakthrough?" Sofia complained.

"Whatever," Sam said as she laid on her bed looking through her emails.

* * *

When they went back to school on Monday, everyone wanted to hang out with them after class.

At recess, a lot of kids crowded around Sam and Sofia, and the twins were pushed back to sit on the seesaw.

"So, can we have a playdate, and maybe see the asteroid?" one asked.

Sofia said, "Nah. The asteroid isn't that cool. Also, I don't know who you are."

But Sam responded with something entirely different: "I'm free after school on Wednesday."

Another person said, "You're so cool since you have an asteroid. Maybe I could see it some time."

"No," Sofia simply answered.

"Maybe some time," Sam would answer.

But Max sat on the soft turf in the corner of the fenced-in playground. He stared at Sam and Sofia. He looked frustrated. Like the twins had stolen something.

"The asteroid isn't that cool. You come to my house, and hang with me," Max said. He waved his muddy brown hair and crossed his arms in the 'cool pose' across his fat chest, then stood up in his spot in the corner. He then put only his thumbs in the pockets of his black leather jacket.

"Yeah, you should hang out with him," Sofia agreed pointing toward Max.

"No, Sofia. It seems like they want to talk about our asteroid," Sam disagreed as she dove into conversation with other people.

"I guess so," Sofia said. She looked at Max and gave Sam a forced smile.

* * *

Sam and Sofia walked through the long halls to humanities class. After humanities ended, they went on with their peaceful day at school.

When school was over, they stayed for a little while because everyone was still asking them about the asteroid. They decided to take advantage of it while they could and enjoy their popular day.

Then they started for home and looked at looked at the fallen leaves, stopping once thinking of the peaceful fall they had. Leaves slowly fell to the ground, and it was like a breathtaking life of swoops in one direction just to be blown in the other. And finally a kid came along and snatched it out of the air. He crushed it as he ran over to the bike rack on the street corner. Sofia and Sam were thinking about how terrible the school day was, and then they felt guilty for thinking this was worse than their mom dying. They both had to wipe a tear off their saddened faces.

"We could take it to the labs, because it has no use to us," Sofia breaking the silence after making sure Sam couldn't see the tear.

Luckily Sam had wiped hers away too. It was in the past. She had died, just like they had cried, and now all they can do is mourn. But not in front of each other of course. "No. We worked hard for it. And if we have it, we'll have friends. Do you want to give that up?" Sam asked now thinking about her terrible day at school as pretty good. When you think about it there were many benefits to the day. And Sam saw those as essential.

"Yes," Sofia said as if it were obvious. "It's kinda the point. And don't you mean popular?"

"Same thing! But I guess we can give it up," Sam admitted sorrowfully. "It's just kind of nice being heard and having an opinion."

"Well, that's one use for it," Sofia said. "But not that good of an *excuse.*"

"We could pretend that it's awesome and it did stuff!" Sam said just throwing ideas out.

"What type of stuff would we say it — oh my gosh! What am I saying? I don't want to lie," Sofia said.

"You're right," Sam said as she looked down. "It's just wrong."

"We might as well smash it," Sofia said. She was angry that the asteroid had made her sister seem so weird.

"That might be a good idea," Sam said with a smile. "There might be something good in there. I saw a pink light shine during the mayor's announcement."

Sofia saw the pink light in her mind, and quickly agreed. "And if there isn't, we won't have to deal with popularity," she said.

"Yeah!" Sam screamed. "Wait," she said more slowly.

"Why are you so obsessed with being popular?" Sofia asked. She looked at Sam with curiosity.

"Who's gonna do it?" Sam asked, changing the conversation.

"Not it!" They answered at the same time as they touched their noses.

"We'll both do it at the same time," Sofia suggested. They walked onto the porch of their white-painted house.

* * *

When they got home, they ran up the creaky stairs to their shared room. They ran over to the asteroid, which rested on the round, pink, furry carpet, in between two neatly made twin beds. The light coming from the window seemed to directly shine on the epic-looking asteroid.

"We need hammers, knives, and shovels," Sam said.

"Oh my," Sofia said. They laughed.

"Now seriously, go get them," Sam told Sofia pointing out the door.

"Okay," Sofia responded in a disgusted type of voice. "Rude," she added. She raced to the bottom of the stairs and searched through the tool closet.

Clank! Clank! Clank!

Sofia went up the stairs, handed Sam the knife, and took the hammer in her hands.

"Three," Sam said.

"Two," Sofia said.

"One," they both said.

CHAPTER 4:

THE MAGIC

They hit it hard. They hit it so many times that Sofia and Sam felt as if their arms were going to fall off.

Both of their foreheads had beads of sweat, and they were breathing deeply.

"Can we take a break?" Sofia asked, panting.

"You can. But I've got a job to finish," Sam answered.

"Well, I can't let you work alone," Sofia said hesitantly. She started up again.

Sam was breathing deeply as she said, "I really wanted to open this stupid rock." But when Sam was about to give up and put the hammer down, she had one last hope. *I don't think this is going to work, so I'll take one last hit. And if I don't make it crack open, I quit.*

This time, Sam was desperate. She went all the way back into a proper position, then ripped it down fast and hit it as hard as it took to break off a piece.

"Good job," Sofia said. Sam continued to look at the break she had made.

"Um … Sofia?" Sam pointed to the spot where the piece broke off. A bright pink light was shining from that small hole. And singing was coming from the asteroid.

Aww…

"What's happening?" Sofia shouted.

The pink light got brighter … and brighter … and brighter, until there was no asteroid, just light. But then it separated into two balls of light.

"Ahh!" Sam and Sofia screamed. The two balls of light looked alike, just like them. They were both round and seemed as if they were just colored air. The light got closer … and closer … and closer. Until it grabbed them. They opened their mouths screaming as if the doctor was checking their throat. Soon the light came in and it was like they could see the light was so bright it had shown through them. It smelled sweet like honey.

They were surrounded by the pink light. It swirled them up into the air. Their hair flowed above their heads, and their clothes changed to what looked like their shade of skin, because the light blocked out the colors of their hair and clothes.

But the scariest thing happened last. Their pupils shrank until all that was left of their eyes were blank white spots.

And then, the light was shrinking … and shrinking … and shrinking, until it was gone.

For a second, their eyes were still white. But with a few blinks, their pupils slowly started to return.

They plunged toward the pink rug in their room. But just a few seconds after they touched the surface, they slowly started lifting again into the air. Yes, they started flying again! Or floating. Right there in the air.

"What. Is. Happening?" they both said. "We're flying!"

CHAPTER 5:

ON MARS

Feria 45, 4005 (September 18, 2018), nine days before Sam and Sofia discovered the asteroid

Once upon a time...

On Mars, there was a village called Marasia. The town was quaint and had lots of cottages. There was a poor and evil girl named Victoria. She lived just outside the village, in the red desert of Cleaminia. Victoria had hair blacker than coal and eyes as green as leaves. She had skin so pale it almost seemed to turn green.

Victoria lived in a small hut made from rocks that fell off the mountain peaks. She had no money, no friends, no anything. It was sad.

Because she was poor, she needed many things she didn't have — or so she thought she needed. Really, what she wanted most was to be the leader of Cleaminia, but she couldn't because of the wretched leader (or so she thought). Victoria wanted to live in the luxurious castle she had heard stories about, the one that looked like a regular house on Earth except it was all made out of stone. If she ruled the land, she would make her subjects give her food. With servants, she wouldn't have to work so hard every day getting groceries for other people from the only garden with oxygen for plants to survive. She has the lowest job in her neighborhood, Grocery Shopper. The town needed a shopper because the grocery store was fifty miles away. Every once in a while, she would go fifty miles, and the rest of the time she would make sure people paid for the food. Being leader would be everything she wanted: shelter, food, and help.

She needed to come up with a good plan.

"I'm tired of living in this giant pile of rubble!" she shouted at the walls as her face turned red. "I need to be the leader, and I need a plan," she said. That had been her hope for a long time, but she thought it probably wouldn't happen.

She spent quite some time thinking about how she could become the leader.

"I could — no," she would say. Or, "How about — wait, how will I get those materials?"

* * *

But one day, she figured it out.

"I could use the legendary asteroid of magic from the crater in the center of Mars. All I need to do is smash it until it opens and then use the magic to take over!" She considered this to be a good plan. The crater was a government-protected area, however, so it wouldn't be taken easily.

The only problem with her plan was that the leader of Cleaminia knew about her plan, by looking through the crystal ball. He wanted to stop it.

"How could that witch do this? I'm the best leader Mars has ever had!" the leader exclaimed. His face turned as red as a pepper. He watched the tape on the magical rock again and double-checked on what he heard. "I haven't said anything about her living on my property, because I don't want her to die. But if she goes through with this plan, then I'll be forced to push Victoria off the property. And she will die."

A knight barged into the leader's chambers. "Leader, what's wrong? I heard you talking to yourself … again."

"Prepare the carriages," the leader said. "And I will talk to myself, because there is an issue. It's not because I have nothing to do with my anger and I'm crazy."

"I never said anything about that," the knight said.

"And now you did. Go get the carriage prepared like I told you to!" the leader shouted.

"On it, sir," the knight said as he looked at the leader with fear and then left the room quickly.

* * *

Victoria went on a long journey to the crater, which was in the center of Mars. In the desert, she met many people that she used to get food.

"Hi. Dear people, I beg of you. Food, please," Victoria said.

"Oh no. Dear husband, we have to give her something," the old lady said.

"I know. Give her the jar of brussel sprouts," the husband said.

The old lady walked slowly with her cane toward the small kitchen, flipped open the rock that covered a hole, and picked out a jar filled with brussel sprouts.

"Here you go," the old lady said when she came back from the kitchen.

"Thank you ever so much for these juicy pleasures," Victoria said as she left through the stone door.

As the door closed behind her, she tossed the jar of brussel sprouts onto the sandy ground and pulled a banana out of her backpack. Victoria had stolen the fruit from the Conserved Gardens, where the couple had probably bought the brussel sprouts. She smiled. Victoria wouldn't have eaten anything they offered her, even if it had been candy. She just wanted them to lose some food.

* * *

As Victoria went along on her journey, she did not know that the Royal Guard were right behind her. The leader didn't want the guards to attack until she reached the crater.

"I can almost envision it in my head, our defeat over that little brat," the leader said. He realized that he could see the crater. If he was that close, so was Victoria. "Almost there," he heard her say.

Victoria broke into a run, and she seemed to be excited to be so close, she just had to sneak by the invisible barrier. It only had one entrance, and the leader was the only soul who was supposed to know it but Victoria had learned it by hearing it from the leader himself (he went to the king asking for a fragment of magic inside, as to cure his 80 year old grandpa of chest pain that was about to kill him).

The leader climbed up from his carriage onto a horse and went faster. It was his mission to catch up with her. "I've got you cornered," he shouted.

Victoria didn't react to his shouting. As she reached the crater, she picked up the asteroid as if she were hugging it. "Finally!"

The leader caught up with her. "I want that rock."

"Never!" she exclaimed. Victoria broke into a run and headed back from where she came.

"Guards!" the leader shouted. The guards came out of hiding behind the rocks and ran toward Victoria. They trapped her and took her to the castle.

* * *

When they got to the castle, the leader asked her a question in the dungeons from across the bars, "What did you think you were going to do?"

"I thought I could use that rock of magic and take over the kingdom with fear," she said menacingly.

"Well, how did that work out then?" the leader asked as he walked back and forth.

"Great, 'til you bratty castle people showed up!" she shouted, following him as he moved.

"Guards," the leader said. The guards opened the cell, ran toward Victoria, and took her away.

"Let go!" Victoria shouted.

"Never!" the guards started running up some stairs with her in their arms. Her hair was tangled, and her clothes were ripped by the roughhousing. The guards followed her.

"Stop. I'll deal with this," the leader said as he walked up the stairs. The guards let go, and she quickly grabbed the asteroid which was heavy. The annoyed Martian ran all around the castle as fast as she could having to push the asteroid. She got to a lab with space equipment, such as rocket ships, a radio station (to communicate), gas, and extra supplies probably in case something were to go missing.

The leader found Victoria where she had stopped to catch her breath. She leaned on the rocket that sat on the launch pad. The leader took this as his chance. He ran into Victoria, stole the asteroid out of her hands, and hugged it under his arms in the same way that she had been doing, and pushed it across the room.

"Give it back!" Victoria exclaimed.

The leader didn't respond. He ran toward the rocket ship and tossed the asteroid into the rocket.

"You wouldn't!" Victoria shouted.

"Blast off!" the leader said as he reached for the launch lever.

But as he was just about to pull down the launch lever, Victoria ran over, pulled a knife out of her bag, and held it against her hand. She held her hand up high, and just as it came crashing down, the leader swiftly pulled down the launch lever.

The leader's body split in two, and the rocket with the asteroid blasted off into space.

"Noo!" Victoria shouted at the top of her lungs. "Why? I put so much effort into it, for nothing! And I lost my chance at becoming the leader, because I will never defeat his army. I guess I will be poor forever."

Then she noticed the leader's remains. Blood was spilling all over his now-split body. She saw the inside organs and how the split made all his digested food come out the wrong way. She saw inside of his brain. The gross juiciness.

She picked up the two pieces of the leader and threw them out a window.

"Eww!" exclaimed someone below the window.

* * *

Now, back to the asteroid. You guessed it. That asteroid was the same one that Sam and Sofia took home.

CHAPTER 6:

WEEKEND'S OVER

The twins were in utter astonishment.

They couldn't comprehend in their heads that they had magic.

"Wow!" They said this at the same time. They were panting repeatedly. It felt like they were eating cotton candy and going into a bone-chilling forest at the same time.

"Okay. I think I got it processed. We have powers. What are we gonna do first?" Sam asked going into a flying pose.

"Hide them!" Sofia responded as her head tilted to the side.

"Why hide them?" Sam asked as she tilted her head to the side to side.

"Because, what if people want our magic? Will they try to take it from us? And if they take it from us, how much pain will we have to bear to give it to them?" Sofia explained as her hands trembled. "I don't want this magic, and you shouldn't want it either."

"Sofia, you're over-exaggerating. And that's not what I meant by 'what are we gonna do first'. I didn't mean anything that would get us in trouble," Sam said. She tried to convince her sister.

"We should still hide it," Sofia said as her eyes opened wider. "Oh, and why are we still floating?"

"Because we can't stop," Sam replied looking up and down.

"We should learn," Sofia suggested as she looked around the room.

"Maybe it just goes at our command," Sam suggested. "Down!" She went up higher and crashed through the roof. "Really?" Sam asked as she brought her hand to her face.

"Maybe, be nicer," Sofia shouted up to Sam. "Try something like, please, can I go down?" She smashed to the floor and through it. "Hi, living room." Sofia shouted more loudly, so Sam could hear the joke.

They giggled a little.

"A combination, maybe?" Sam said. "Down." This time, she didn't shout. Gently, she went down through the gap in the ceiling and onto the floor. "I found out what works!" she yelled through the hole in the floor.

"Great!" Sofia shouted. "Now fix the hole in the ceiling. And don't try to use it while we're in school, at home, or on the streets."

"Okay," Sam didn't know if this would work her not. She had to go by her instincts. She pointed up and thought about the hole being fixed. She must have closed her eyes because she had to open them. The hole in the ceiling was gone.

"So, basically we can never use our powers?" Sam asked getting off the topic. "Also, you fix this hole," Sam pointed at the hole right next to her. She watched as Sofia went through the same process as she did. Sam ran down the stairs.

"Answering your previous question, yeah we pretty much can't use our powers ever," Sofia replied as they both sat on the couch and turned on the large TV.

* * *

The next day, they went to school and pretended that everything was fine. They sat on the benches outside of school.

"I *so* want to mention I have powers," Sam whispered to Sofia. "We'll be the most popular kids in school, maybe even the world."

"No! We'll be the *least* popular," Sofia said as she looked at Sam.

"Why would that be?" Sam asked as she put her hands on her hips.

"Okay Mrs. Sassy! Because scientists will want to do tests on us, and we won't be *able* to go to school," Sofia explained, scared by what she was saying. Sofia felt a tingling in her hand. "Ow," she whispered under her breath.

"Fine. Let's talk about something else then," Sam suggested. "Have you noticed that even though we have the asteroid, people aren't talking to us, or about us? What if they know that we're not gonna let them see it?"

"Maybe," Sofia said, "but even if we aren't popular anymore, why does it matter? I mean, we never expected it, wanted it, or even liked it."

"That's what you think," Sam said as she walked into school across the brick ground. Sofia followed her and brought her back to the benches.

A few seconds later, Max showed up and saw them talking. "Are you talking about how you went from Most-Popular-Kid-in-School back to Least-Popular-Kid-in-School?" Max asked looking at them in disgust. "It's because I saw you earlier through your window, and I didn't see any asteroid."

"You're so dramatic. And why were you spying on us anyway?" Sofia asked a little disgusted.

"So I could see if the asteroid did stuff. Duh," Max said as he pulled his hands up from his head.

"Well, it didn't," Sofia said quickly.

"What did it do?" Max asked excitedly. He stared at Sofia with eyes full of hope.

"We're being serious," Sam said. She tried to sound like there was nothing to hide. "Now, go away and mope in your little corner over there," Sam said, making fun of Max as she pointed toward the corner and walked away.

Max walked away and sat on the hard, black, cement ground.

Sam laughed as she stopped in the middle of the playground.

"That wasn't nice," Sofia said.

"At least we got payback," Sam responded.

"We should go say sorry. We're being just as bad as he is," Sofia said.

"What did I tell you about saying sorry to Max?" Sam asked.

"That sorry is just what he wants, and he's just trying to get his popularity back," Sofia said accurately before adding: "But that's not what matters right now. It's this: say sorry, and do *not* be as bad as he is and feel really bad in the end." She was clenching her fist. "It'll be good for you and Max if you say sorry. You won't feel bad, which I know you do. Is it worth it, to feel this bad just to be popular?" Sofia's hand trembled in pain a little bit.

"No!" Sam shouted as if she was going to say yes. "Yes? I don't know. I just want to be popular. And I feel like the way he became popular is easy and works." She was torn. "But deep down, I also feel bad and want to say sorry. I just don't know why I'm torn. It's such a trivial and useless topic."

"Say sorry," Sofia said softly and sweetly as she pointed toward Max.

"Okay," Sam said, feeling a little better as she took a deep breath.

They walked over the dark black cement to the corner where Max sat on the ground in front of the tall metal fence and talked with his friends.

"What do you want?" Max asked, mid-conversation with his friends as he turned toward Sam.

"To say sorry," Sofia said looking him straight in the eyes. "For being mean to you all the time."

Max laughed, then looked at their faces and saw the twins' serious, blank expressions. "Oh. You're serious."

Sofia looked at his friends. "Can you leave?" she asked. They started walking toward the play structure and sat on the seesaw.

"Of course we are," Sam said regretting it as soon as the words came out of her mouth. *I didn't want to be saying that about actually being sorry, or anything else. I want him to cry, and I want to fly.* Sam had that cry and fly part in her head for days and planned to memorize it so she could say it when she had the chance. "I'm sorry for everything." Sam sounded serious. But in her mind she thought, *I would never say this to Max. Too bad I have such a weirdly nice twin. I want a twin who agrees to everything I want or say.*

In her head, Sam imagined that she was walking by Max to get to the other girls who were talking and leaning on the play structure. As she passed Max, she would say, "Missing your friends? Well, here they are. Go talk to them." Then she'd wave her hand to the girls.

And Max would say, "Grrr," sounding like the dog Sam thought he was.

She came back to reality looking nervously in her twin's direction, and Sofia gave Sam a thumbs up. Then Sam imagined herself laughing and turning around as she waved to the girls talking and leaning against the play structure. But as Sam was imagining, something interrupted her thoughts.

"Sam? Sam? Sam?" Sofia waved her hand in front of Sam's face.

"I'm alive. What's going on?" Sam asked.

"You dazed out," Sofia said.

"Right when I was doing my speech, or whatever you would call it, about how I felt about you making fun of me!" Max said. "I am *not* forgiving this jerk!" Max walked away, over to his friends on the seesaw.

"Sorry," Sam said as she looked at Sofia.

"Nope. You were the one who thought that this was a joke. Now I *really* hope that you get that guilty feeling. But it shouldn't be me you're saying sorry to. You should have heard his speech."

CHAPTER 7:

HOW THE HAG DID SHE GET THERE?

Victoria looked out onto the stone walls and cell bars of the prison of the castle Cleaminia.

The worst part about being in the dungeon was that she had a roommate ... who was a troll ... who always sobbed about it being unfair that she was in the dungeon.

"So, my father was standing there, to show where they should land the foundation stone, and the worker from Bob's Construction was about to hit the lever to drop the foundation stone," the troll said. She stopped talking to blow her nose on Victoria's shirt. "And I ran toward the crane that was about to drop it, and I tore off the piece of the metal shell protecting the cords. I started ripping at the cords to stop the crane from putting the stone down. So, you see, I was only trying to help my father."

"But there were many ways to get your Dad out of there," Victoria said. "You could have warned him to run out, shout to the construction workers 'Hey, that's my Dad in that ditch', or even-"

"No that was the only thing to do," the troll said, jumping repeatedly, making the cell shake. "And I *definitely* knew of those other choices and *did* think of them."

"Whatever. You – " Victoria was about to say something but stopped. "OMSG!" (The S is for space, so together it's Oh My Space God.) "I'm comforting a dumb troll!"

"Hey!" the troll said, sounding offended and slapped her.

"Ow! Like you don't know it's true," Victoria yelled in pain as she looked to the large troll with resent on the edge of her lip.

"I'm *glad* you're gonna die now," the troll said crossing her arms.

"Did you say gonna *die*?" Victoria asked standing up from the stone floor.

"Yeah. Everyone in the dungeons dies when the month ends. There are so many criminals on Mars, they need more spaces by next month," the troll explained wiping the tears from her face.

"It's Feria the 47th!" Victoria said, panicked. "The last day of Feria."

"Exactly," the troll said.

* * *

Later that day, all the cells were open, and Victoria knew why: they were going to die. She was devastated.

Everyone walked through the hallway that led to the entrance. Victoria was looking at the ground and walking in the chains that held her arms together. At first, the ground was black and made of bricks. Then they went through the castle hallway and saw marble, the rarest rocks could only belong to the leader. But Victoria had killed the leader. So, now, the Queen was the leader. Marble, the rarest of rocks could only belong to the *Queen*. Victoria and the other prisoners went through the front door of the castle and saw red rock.

A huge crowd was cheering.

Victoria looked ahead and saw a line of people. But she didn't see *that* many people. Why did the Queen have to kill everyone once a month? Then she looked behind her. The line went beyond her view, and faded as it reached over the mounds in the distance. Oh. People.

The first person in line walked up the stone stairs. Once he got to the top, the attendant knight put the prisoner's head in the hole in the guillotine.

"What was your offense?" the Queen asked sitting in a chair made of marble. She was mainly looking at her outfit of leaves, likely made from plants at the Conserved Gardens—the only spots on Mars that can have plants.

"I stole from the closet in your room yesterday," the criminal said.

"And you want to say?" the Queen asked holding a crown of rock, that he had probably stolen.

"Sorry," the criminal said as his voice went higher pitched. He looked down.

"Well, if I hear it like that, I have no choice. All I can say is, drop it down guards!" the Queen shouted looking straight at the person about to have his head cut off.

The guards let go of the rope that kept the knife at the top. The blade dropped down speedily and quickly. Victoria only saw the blood that spattered onto her feet. It was as if someone shot an arrow through some cranberry juice. Victoria didn't mind though. She was going to die anyway.

The same routine happened to everyone in front of her. Offense, apology, drop, splattered cranberry juice. Victoria wondered if each person hoped that their response would stop the blade from dropping. She certainly hoped hers did. She didn't want to be cranberry juice.

Soon, it was Victoria's turn. Victoria's head was forced into the guillotine. She couldn't look up at the Queen, which she was happy about because she didn't want people to remember her as a crying, sensitive freak.

"What was your offense?" the Queen asked.

"I killed the last leader," Victoria said.

"And you want to – wait! What?" the Queen shouted. "You *killed* the last leader?"

"Yes," Victoria said, and she heard everyone gasp.

"And you want to say?" The Queen ignored what she said before.

"I don't regret it," Victoria said. She heard more gasps as she shocked everyone again.

"Well, when you say it like that, I have no choice. All I can say is, next one up."

"What?" Victoria asked as the guards took her out of the machine.

"I hated the leader," the Queen said. "He always was so mean to me. *I* was the older sibling, but our parents wanted a boy leader." The Queen's voice was getting deeper, and her face was turning red.

"Oh. So you wanted to be Queen?" Victoria asked relating to her ambition.

"Exactly. And you made it happen," the Queen said. She pointed over to sit on the side lines. "Thank you. So, because you made my dream come true, whatever you want will be yours."

"I do want a space rocket," Victoria said as she sat down on the now comfortable rock.

"Then it is yours. Where do you want to go?" the Queen asked kindly.

"I had an asteroid that was mine, but the leader took it away and sent it away to another place. I don't know where it is. Can you show me where the asteroid is located, so I can rocket to wherever it is?" Victoria asked.

"Okay," the Queen said. "Guards, finish up the rest of them." She pointed to Victoria. "Follow me."

"Coming."

* * *

They walked toward the launching room, where the old leader had blasted the asteroid into space. Then they walked over to the computer in the corner.

"Let's check the last shuttle that went into space," the Queen said as she began typing on the loud computer. *Click, click, click.* "Was this it?"

"Yes."

"Now let's look at the tracking device that was on that rocket," the Queen said.

Click, click, click. An arrow pointed from Mars to just outside a green, blue, and yellowish sand-colored planet.

"It looks like it was just outside planet Earth, but then either lost connection or exploded," the Queen explained. "So, is that where you want to go? Earth?"

"Wait," Victoria said realizing how fast the rocket had to have gone. "How did it get there so fast?"

"We have a magic orb, from our first Queen. We have a little bit of magic in every rocket, making it go *really* fast."

"Where is the orb?" Victoria asked thinking that maybe she could have magic.

"In the main hall," the Queen replied, "Why?"

"No reason," Victoria responded greedily. "I need to go to the bathroom."

"Then go," the Queen said. "Third door on the right."

Victoria ran to the bathroom and opened the door. But when the Queen was looking somewhere else, she ran through the hall. Victoria curved around corners and tried to find the main hall. Once she found it, she barely noticed the suits of armor lining the walls. Her gaze was focused on a stand in the center. A magical orb glowed from inside a case on the stand.

"There it is," she whispered. She slowly tried to take off the case. "Dang it!" The case had a retina scanner.

As she thought about what to do next, Victoria saw the swords that the suits of armor were holding down. "Ah ha," Victoria said. She ran over and grabbed one of the swords. Then she rushed back to the case with the orb and held the sword up high.

A computer voice interrupted Victoria's plan. "Correct sword. Access accepted."

She put down the sword and removed the case. After she put the case on the floor, she reached her hand out for the orb. As the glow faded, the magic also started to vanish. Victoria felt a small sting and dropped the orb. She thought of killing the rest of the criminals later.

"I have powers," Victoria said happily. "I think."

She ran and put the sword back with the suit of armor, then raced through the hall to get back to the space rocket control room.

"I'm ready," Victoria said. She was out of breath.

"Then get ready for takeoff," the Queen said. She pointed toward the rocket on the platform.

Victoria got in the rocket and tightly closed the door.

"Turn on pilot from lab," the Queen said to her computer.

Victoria put her seatbelt on and said, "Ready."

The Queen pulled down levers until she got to the last one (which just happened to be red). She said, "Blast off!"

CHAPTER 8:

ON THAT ROCKET

You're probably wondering what happened on the rocket holding the asteroid.

As the rocket went through space, it passed lots of meteorites and pretty places, like those you see when you look up pictures of galaxies.

No one guided this rocket to anywhere, so it was just barreling along to Earth, using a jagged and awkward route. It approached Earth at a very fast speed.

Martian instruments indicated a huge asteroid was on a path to crash into the rocket's skin. A few days later, however, the rocket was in Earth's atmosphere and seemed to be moving through it.

But the wiring system broke. The blasters slowed down until they were as slow as a snail crawling across the ground. Then the blasters were completely cut off. They looked like a dog had chewed on them. But there was another problem. The ship was overheated.

The broken wires burst into sparks, and the rocket's heat made the sparks catch on fire. Soon, red and orange flames covered the ship. The red was like a tart red apple, and the orange looked just like a construction cone flashing in the middle of the road. The rocket was on fire.

Blazing orange flames started to creep up the side of the ship ... on the side with the fuel tank.

The fuel started to leak, and the flames took over and obliterated the ship until ... the ship exploded.

But the asteroid didn't break. It hurled toward Earth. Gravity completely took over the asteroid, and it landed in the streets of Miami.

There seemed to be millions of people rushing toward the small asteroid.

CHAPTER 9:

DISCOVERING POSSIBILITIES

Sam and Sofia were walking through a park on their way home from school.

"Sofia, don't you think it might be fun if we did stuff with our powers? Like maybe learn what powers we have and use them to do stuff?" Sam asked curiously. "Cause I want to fly fast and feel the wind in my hair, for fun." Sam pretended to fly on their neighbor's lawn.

"No!" Sofia responded loudly. "We might get caught."

"But what if we go out to sea and do it?" Sam suggested. "No one will see us."

"Boaters," Sofia said thinking of reasons.

"Oh, yeah. Right," Sam said sarcastically. "Can we at least go out and see what we can do, find out the limits of our powers?"

"Okay, fine. But don't make me regret it," Sofia responded pointing a finger at her.

Suddenly, a dark, shadowy figure came hurtling toward Sam. "Ahh!" she screamed. "What is this?"

"A chipmunk!"

* * *

"Good night," Dad said as he walked back to the door after kissing the girls on the cheek.

"'Night," Sam said pulling up the covers.

"Good night," Sofia said sweetly turning off the light. The room went dark.

Their Dad stepped out of the room and closed the door.

Sofia and Sam waited to hear Dad's footsteps stop, which would mean he was in his room.

Step, step, step ... click!

"He's in his room, with the door shut," Sam whispered getting out of her bed.

"I still regret going," Sofia whispered, "but I'll go. I promised."

The two crept down the stairs. Some of the steps croaked like a hungry frog, but the door to Dad's bedroom stayed shut. They walked through the front door and felt the cool night air on their faces.

"This way toward the beach," Sofia said, doubting herself.

They walked through the empty streets, on the outskirts of the city. The street lanterns guided their way.

"It's creepy at night, with no people or light. Like a ghost town," Sam said staying in the center of the sidewalk and looking around.

"I know," Sofia responded.

"Let's just hurry and get there," Sam said.

They ran down the sidewalks toward the beach. When they reached the beach, they jumped down off the wood boardwalk onto the blue-yellow-looking sand. The blue came from the shade of the dark night. They looked at the water, which was dark blue and a little scary.

"Let's go out there," Sam said. "How do we do that?"

"Didn't you figure out how to in the beginning?" Sofia asked.

"Oh, right. We demand nicely, but not too nicely," Sam said.

"Okay," Sofia responded. "Fly."

"Fly," Sam said after Sofia raised into the air. "This is still *so* cool."

"Let's go out before we get caught," Sofia said in a rushed voice. "Forward."

"Forward," Sam said.

They shot forward, way too fast to see anything, way too fast for anyone to see them.

"Stop!" Sofia shouted.

She didn't stop.

"You have to do it nicely," Sam explained, again.

"Well, it's hard when you feel like your gonna *die*!" Sofia said in a 'really, you don't know this' voice.

"Stop," they both said calmly, even though they felt like screaming on the inside.

"Okay, I didn't think we'd go at light speed," Sam said as she apologized.

"I think we went around the world. Three times," Sofia joked.

Sam laughed.

"Now that I think about it, we might actually have," Sofia said, thinking.

"Okay, let's start again," Sam said. "So, how do we figure this out?"

"Uhm ..." Sofia wondered. "Maybe our powers could help us." Her voice was sarcastic.

They laughed.

"Oh, wait. When you had the idea to crush the asteroid, this whole magic thing happened. So it might actually work," Sam said pointing at Sofia. "Oh, all powerful powers, please teach us how our blessed powers work."

"Really?" Sofia said in a know-it-all voice.

A spirit-looking ghost showed up. The spirit had stone bluish skin and hair a vibrant green. The hair was so long it dipped into the ocean, down to the point where they couldn't see it anymore. Her nose was flat, like a bunch of sheets of paper. The creepiest part was that her eyes had no pupils, just a black outline.

"You needed help?" the spirit said in a ghostly voice opening its rock mouth slowly.

"Yes, we want to know how our powers work," Sam said, looking up at, it jittering a bit now.

"Sit down," the spirit said as a room appeared around them that looked like it might be in a genie's lantern.

Sam and Sofia walked across the tile floor and sat on the gold-colored chairs. The floor caught their eyes; it had special markings on it. There was a heart and a star overlapping. Then they looked up and saw the spirit sitting in a large purple and gold throne in front of them.

"So, what you want to know is how your powers work?" the spirit asked.

"Yes," Sofia said still concentrating on the floor.

"If you must know, you have to hear the story of how the magic was made. It is part of why the magic works in this way," the spirit said mystically. "My name Zambezi."

"Mine is Sofia, and hers is Sam," Sofia said pointing at Sam.

"I know," the spirit said looking down at them with a smile on its face.

This response was creeping out Sofia and Sam.

"I've known you for a long time. I am your magic. Well, I was made from your magic."

"So, back to the story," Sam said, desperate to learn something.

"Okay, let's begin. *Once upon a time ...*"

* * *

"There was a girl. She was very selfish. So selfish that if she had a choice to give her best friend a dollar or else die, she wouldn't give it to her," the spirit said.

"One day, while she was walking through the streets of Paris on her vacation, she was kidnapped. The kidnapper took her to the trash landfill. He took her into a building that was a fort made from trash and dumped her out of the bag she was in.

"She was scared. The kidnapper took off his black mask, revealing he was a man. He said, 'Kids ruined my life.' He complained, 'They drained my money. My kids decided to waste all my money on getting their own whatever technology. Oh, and also they killed my wife' the guy explained. 'So now, I'll destroy you, a kid. Happy all the time, without the pressure of being an adult.'

"He went to the other side of the trash room and picked up a knife. The girl was so scared she stopped breathing. He came back over, raised the knife above the girl's head, and was about to bring it crashing down. But just at the last moment, a boy came out from a pile of trash and stopped the knife from hitting her head. 'You!' the guy said angrily. 'Yes, me. I know that you're mad at children, but that doesn't give you the excuse to kill them, Uncle Henry,' the boy said. He threw the knife out of the fort.

"'Fine, I'll stop taking my anger out on the wrong people.' Henry said, 'Just let me get it so I can tell the trash people to destroy it,' Henry said. He walked toward the door where the knife landed, and once it was in his hand, he ran toward the boy who interrupted and crashed the knife into his head." The spirit paused, then continued.

"But that boy had saved many more people, risking his life many times. This was the only time he died in the process. But he didn't completely die. He turned into a star, because he was such a great person. But he wasn't just a star. He gained magical powers as a star. For his kindness.

"One day, an asteroid crashed right into the star. The asteroid broke open, and the powers were absorbed into the asteroid. Then the asteroid sealed itself up. That asteroid kept moving. It moved to Mars and created a crater.

"You may be wondering how the asteroid ended up on Earth, then? Recently, a rocket with that asteroid in it took off from Mars and exploded. And that's what happened to your asteroid," Zambezi said.

"But how does that explain how our powers work?" Sofia asked, wanting to get this over with.

"I forgot a part. Each time the boy saved a person, he created a bit of magic. But that magic has to stay together or else it's just tiny bits of magic that don't work. So, your powers can create new powers all the time. But it won't work if you are fighting. And you can never, not ever, use your powers against blood. If you do, you will both lose your powers, and your enemies will be upon you. Well, other than using normal powers like levitating different objects, but not people," Zambezi explained expressionless.

"Okay. But why did you have to tell us the story?" Sam asked looking at her curiously.

"If I didn't tell you, you would be asking for the story," Zambezi said as if she had done this before.

"She's got a point," Sofia said looking to Sam. "Thank you for the info about our powers."

"It's almost morning. Now be gone with you," Zambezi said as she waved her hands.

They were flying at light speed again, until they reached their home and were tucked into their beds.

"I'll let you do anything," Sam said. "I trust you."

"Me, too."

CHAPTER 10:

COMING TO EARTH

"We're almost there," the Queen said to Victoria over the contact speaker.

"Got it," Victoria replied. Victoria was hypnotized by the beauty outside the large window. The pretty galaxies caught her eye over and over. "Give me some information about Earth," Victoria said as she saw the planet out the window.

"Well, Earth has people like we do, but the people are different. They breathe oxygen instead of carbon dioxide, so breathing might feel a little weird," the Queen said.

"And?" Victoria asked.

"It also has liquid," the Queen said.

"What's liquid?" Victoria asked.

"It's a ... well, it ... it's hard to describe," the Queen stumbled as she spoke.

"Anything else I *need* to know?" Victoria asked.

"They have way more people," the Queen warned. "Stay away from them, unless you have to go near the person who has what you want."

"Okay, I'm ready. Approximately where on the Earth did the asteroid land?" Victoria asked.

"Our cameras don't go that far, so you'll have to look," the Queen said.

"*Look?* Have you seen this planet? It's bigger than Mars," Victoria complained.

"Oh. Well, there's nothing I can do," the Queen said in a sorry voice.

"There must be something," Victoria said getting louder.

"Well, I can tell you about the last things it said," the Queen said turning on a recording. "This rocket looks a little weird. I mean, it doesn't look like the ones that are normally in the USA."

"So, I just have to find the USA and look around there? That's better. Depending on the size of the USA," Victoria said hopefully.

"So, you ready to land?" the Queen asked.

"Okay," Victoria said, "but please, don't go too fast, like when we took off."

"Sorry, impossible," the Queen said pressing a few buttons. "Now, buckle up."

The rocket was zooming once again. The artificial gravity switch was turned on, so at least Victoria wasn't flying and hitting the side of the ship. She looked out the window and saw flames on the side of the ship. "Uhm, are there supposed to be flames?" Victoria asked.

"Yes, it's totally normal," the Queen said, "as long as they're not on the inside."

"Good," Victoria said, relieved.

Meanwhile, on the outside, the flames were getting close to the window. The frame of the window started turning black

... then it went further in ... and even further... then, the window was covered in black. From the center, the material in the window was caving in. The window was melting.

"Uhm ... the fire is melting the window," Victoria said frantically speaking into to contact speaker. "Now, I'm no rocket scientist, but I don't think *that* is supposed to happen."

"You're right," the Queen said. "We better get you down there quick, before the fire gets in the rocket or the unbreathable air comes in."

"Unbreathable!" Victoria shouted, scared.

"Yeah. The air is thin up high above the Earth, because oxygen and carbon dioxide are heavy. They go to the bottom, so high up is the weakest amount," the Queen explained. "Now, let me get you going faster."

Victoria felt the rocket jerk a little faster. Then she saw a place with yellow grounds with a moving blue-type thing. People were playing on it.

"What is that?" Victoria muttered to herself.

As the rocket got closer, she saw more clearly that the yellow ground could be separated. She aimed directly for the moving blue part and got closer, but then there was a gust of wind.

The rocket kept going down, then slammed directly in the sand. Victoria slammed head first out of the rocket, and her head went directly into the yellow ground.

"Really?" Victoria shouted, annoyed.

"Who are you? And why did you fall out of the sky?" a little boy asked.

"That doesn't matter," Victoria said gruffly. "Where's the USA?"

CHAPTER 11:

TAKING ADVANTAGE

"Good morning," Sofia said walking down the stairs quickly.

"Hey," Sam said following Sofia.

"Who wants to go to the amusement park?" Dad said in a high pitched voice, getting his keys.

"Don't we have school?" Sam asked picking up her backpack.

"No, silly. It's parent teacher conferences," Dad said pulling out a calendar.

"Aren't *you* a parent?" Sofia asked tilting her head.

"My day to conference is tomorrow," Dad said matter-of-factly.

"'Kay, let's go!" Sam said excitedly.

The two went through their closet, ate a quick breakfast, and brushed their teeth, and hair. Sam screamed a bit while getting a big knot out of her hair.

Rustle, rustle, rustle.

Munch, munch, munch.

Whish, whish, whish.

Oww!

They ran from the doorway where they were standing and jumped into Dad's red convertible. The seats were a light tan leather, the optional roof of the car was brown, the mirrors were small circles, and the steering wheel was a dark brown.

Vroom, vroom, vroom.

The car started. They went down the road, slowly, with a little bit of gas coming out from the back. They went on the highway, took the exit, and zoomed a mile above the speed limit the rest of the way.

"Are we almost there?" Sam asked looking as if she had to pee.

"Yeah, honey. Just three blocks away," Dad said looking to his GPS.

"Sam, since we have our powers and all, you don't wanna do stuff with them. Right?" Sofia whispered thinking about her sister winning all the prizes.

"Are you kidding me?" Sam whispered back a little louder. "That's the only reason I want to go."

"Don't do it," Sofia whispered raising a finger.

"Don't do what?" Sam asked at a normal volume.

"Don't do anything," Sofia replied raising and lowering her hand, trying to get her to quiet down.

"Why?" Sam asked a little quieter again.

"Do I have to tell you again?" Sofia whispered, sounding annoyed.

"Yes," Sam replied trying to get her to just keep chatting.

"What if someone sees us?" Sofia asked. "What will they want to do to us?"

"Uhm …" Sam stumbled.

"Exactly," Sofia said, looking mad as she turned back around to face the chair in front of her. Sam pulled her back.

"That is so not true," Sam said edgily. "I just don't know why."

"Just don't do anything," Sofia repeated, again moving back to the position looking at the chair in front of her.

"We're here," Dad said in a sing-song way.

In front of them was a typical amusement park, with an entrance that was like a sign and a Ferris wheel splat in the middle. There were lots of candy-based carts and buildings with games in them and all sorts of prizes. And then there were the rides. One as tall as a small skyscraper was spinning in upside-down to right-side-up circles and looked scary, yet fun.

"Let's go do the ring toss first," Sam said, pulling the wrists of her dad and sister toward the little building.

They got to the stand and saw rings scattered on the floor of the building. They saw empty bottles that looked like glass but were probably plastic.

"$3 for three rings, and $5 for six!" the host yelled. She smiled at them.

"Get the $5 one," Sam said looking up at Dad, "please."

"Fine," Dad replied, "but can we please get the two? It's cheaper."

"No, it's not," Sam said looking to Sofia. "Not if Sofia plays."

"I guess you're right," Dad said, checking the math in his head. "Let's go."

"$3 for three -"

"Can we get the 5?" Dad asked interrupting the loud ring man.

"Why, of course!" The ring man shouted, throwing his hands up, "I'll just have to take that $5, now."

Dad got his wallet out of his pocket and took out his credit card.

"Do you accept credit cards?" Dad asked handing it to him.

"Sure. Now, just let me swipe the card," the ring man said cheerfully. The ring man walked to the back of the building, went up to the swipe machine and swiped the card.

But Sam noticed that the ring man was no longer smiling. It was like he was faking it. Maybe he was.

The ring man got back, and the fake smile was back on his face. "Here's your credit card," the ring man said carrying the credit card and six rings. "And here are your rings!"

"Let's toss," Sam said picking up three.

Sam threw her first ring a little out of bounds. It wasn't going to hit a single bottle, when suddenly, the ring went back on track and hit the jackpot bottle.

"Lucky on the wind there," the ring man congratulated.

"I pick…" Sam began looking at the selection of prizes.

"What did you do?" Sofia whispered getting closer to Sam.

"I'm getting my prize," Sam said looking at the prizes.

"Did you use your magic?" Sofia asked picturing the scene in her mind.

"So what if I did?" Sam whispered back, and then stood straight to look at the prizes.

"Just don't do it again," Sofia ordered picking up her finger.

"I can't promise that," Sam said. "So I pick, hmm. How about the panda."

"Good choice," the ring man said, "but that was only one of your rings. you have to throw the rest, and she has to throw hers too." The ring man pointed to Sofia.

Sofia tossed her ring right above the bottles, but it went too far.

"Try again," the host said. "You'll get it this time."

Sofia threw it again. Again, it had perfect aim, but this time the ring went too short.

"Great aimer," the host complimented, "just not so good on speed. Last chance try again."

"Okay," Sofia said.

Sofia threw it again. This time the ring went a little off track, but it barely caught on the corner bottle.

"Yay!" Sofia shouted, "and I did it *myself*." She looked at Sam. Sam threw hers, but she probably missed them on purpose.

"I'll have the… how about… "

"Just pick one already, so we can get cotton candy!" Sam shouted picking up her panda.

"Fine. I'll take the little teddy bear," Sofia said. The ring man took the teddy bear, and gave it to Sofia.

"Ha. A little teddy bear can't even match my larger panda," Sam said, trying to make Sofia jealous. "Now for cotton candy."

* * *

They all walked toward the cotton candy machine. The seller said, "Buy one, get one free."

"That's perfect for you two," Dad said smiling.

They got in the long line and waited for about five minutes.

"When is this line gonna end?" Sam complained dragging her feet.

"I'll take one cotton candy, and I'll also take the free one that goes with it," Dad said. "Do you accept credit cards?"

"We do indeed," the seller said, bringing out the card machine. "Let me just add what you want."

"Uhh," Sam complained, looking at the seller who was extremely slow. She leaned down, and her golden-blonde hair almost touched the ground. "It seems like there is *always* something we have to do before we get what we want. Standing in line, running out of cotton candy mix, now waiting for our orders to get on the machine."

"Don't worry, honey," the seller said. "Almost done." The seller typed faster. Way faster. His little fingers seemed to go everywhere at once. "And, done."

"Here you go," Dad said as he handed over the credit card, "and sorry for all that pressure."

"Don't sweat it," the seller said, sweating himself. "It happens all the time."

The seller got two sticks of paper out and whipped them through the cotton candy pot. "One for you," the seller said as he handed the cotton candy to Sofia. "And one for you."

"Thank you," Sofia said to the seller.

"Thanks," Sam said, "for being a slow poke," she added as she turned away. She quickly flicked her fingers to the seller, and he instantly smiled, as if Sam had done a spell.

"Why are you so impatient?" Dad asked, who hadn't forgotten.

"Because I want my cotton candy," Sam replied in a "duh" voice.

"Well, I don't like this attitude, young lady," Dad said firmly, as he pulled out his finger. "One more moment of acting up, and the circus is closed."

"Actually, the circus is open 'til 12 in the morning," Sofia said.

"That's not what I meant," Dad said.

"Let's just take a break and eat our cotton candy," Sam said, and then flicked at Dad too.

They walked toward their car and sat down in it to eat their cotton candy.

Sam was eating it fast. She kept chewing until it was all gone. Then, like magic, the whole thing reappeared.

"What are you doing?" Sofia whispered, leaning to her.

"Didn't I tell you I wanted to use magic?" Sam whispered, thinking of the car conversation.

"Yes, but don't take it overboard," Sofia whispered back. "That probably has no nutrients that the human body needs."

"Don't you get it?" Sam asked. "We're *not* humans."

"Why *wouldn't* we be?" Sofia asked. "We have organs, bones, and all the other stuff!"

"Because we have magic. We're magical people, that's just what we are," Sam said.

"Fine. But we don't have to use it so much we get caught," Sofia whispered. She saw a person on stilts in the corner of her eye and she ran over there, giving Sam the option to do whatever she wanted.

"Whatever," Sam said as she turned her cotton candy, again, into what it was at first.

"Didn't you finish?" Dad asked looking to the recovered cotton candy.

"Yes," Sam said, focusing on her cotton candy.

"How?" Dad asked getting louder.

"Because we have magical powers, that we didn't tell you about," Sam said looking at him now.

"Really?" Dad asked scooting away now.

"No!" Sam said then flicked at him again.

* * *

Once Sam recreated her cotton candy several times (always going through the same routine) they decided to go on the Ferris wheel.

"Which way is the Ferris wheel?" Sam asked.

"That way, where you see the giant one. Right in the middle," Sofia said.

"Let's go," Sam said, excited.

They walked through the crowd of people.

"Excuse me," Sofia said.

"Sorry," Sam said.

They got to the Ferris wheel, and the man handing out the tickets had three more tickets in hand.

"Sir, please give us those tickets. My daughter *really* wants to go on this ride," Dad pleaded.

"Can't just give it to you for free, can I?" the man asked. Dad looked at the sign and it said $15.

"Here's $20," Dad said, handing him a crisp $20 bill from his wallet.

"I'll take it," the man said. He took the money, handed Dad his change, and gave Dad his tickets.

"Thanks," Dad said.

"No problem," the man said cheerfully.

They walked over to the line. When they got there, they waited behind maybe 20 people. They looked at the wheel, going round and round. It slowly came to a stop, then one person got onto the platform and stepped into the cart. It moved a little, then stopped again, and another person got on the next cart.

The line kept going, until it was their turn. They got on the cart, and the wheel started moving, for good.

"This is kinda boring," Sam whispered to Sofia.

"You're not planning to ...?" Sofia got cut off.

"Oh, you know I am," Sam whispered, oddly.

Sam curled her hand, and a little bit of pink came out. The Ferris wheel started to speed up, then popped off the tower.

Creak

The Ferris wheel rolled through the amusement park.

"Ahh!" everyone screamed as they ran out to the street.

Dad's screaming rang through Sam's ear like a siren.

"I told you not to do it," Sofia shouted in a scared voice.

"I know," Sam admitted. "I should have listened."

"Now reverse the spell," Sofia demanded.

"Okay!" Sam shouted. She curled her hands and reversed the spell. Everything started floating. It all went back to how it was before the spell was cast, including everyone's memories.

Whish

If you were really looking, you could see the sun come up a bit.

"Thank you," Sofia said.

"You're welcome," Sam responded.

Dad said, "How's the ride?"

CHAPTER 12:

THE JOURNEY

"I said, where is the USA?" Victoria said holding up a fist. "So, where is it?"

"It- uh-ahh!" the little boy screamed, said a few words in an Australian accent, and ran behind a gray rock.

"I'm sorry," said a woman. She seemed to be the little boy's mom. "Who are you?"

"My name is Victoria. Where is the USA?"

"We're in Australia," the woman said putting her hands up and down.

"And that helps me get to the USA, how?" Victoria asked lowering her head to her shoulder.

"Do you have any money?" the woman asked bringing out a blue thing, with blue and red things sticking out.

"Why does this help me?" Victoria asked looking at the blue thing. "And what is money?"

"You need money to get to the USA, you know?" the woman said getting one of the pieces of paper. It was blue.

"Of course," Victoria lied quickly.

"And money is a currency, something that we Australians use to pay for things, like buying food," the woman explained backing away.

"So where can I go get some *money*?" Victoria asked looking at her confused.

"Well," the woman hesitated still backing away. "There's an opening at that fast food restaurant." She pointed to a large green B across the street.

"Thanks," Victoria said gruffly. She paid no attention to the sandy beach and the bluish-green water. Turning around, she started to walk across the road. In the middle of the street, there was a sign had a red color pointing at her and a green color facing the cars up ahead. She remembered back on Mars how red meant go, and green meant wait thirty seconds. She was sure it hadn't been thirty seconds for the other person, because one had not yet arrived.

A car came barreling on the left side of the yellow line. It raced right in front of Victoria.

"Hey! Don't you ever see a Mar ... er." Victoria stopped herself. "I mean, human?"

"Don't *you* see that a red light is pointing at you?" yelled the driver, a girl who looked old enough to be in college.

"Uhh, whatever," Victoria muttered as she went on with her walk.

She kind of felt *weird*. She felt like a little thing tickled her throat, stomach, and mouth. Maybe it was because she breathed carbon dioxide, and people here breathed oxygen.

Finally, she stood in front of the big B. She read a sign in the window.

Hey Readers!

Need a job?

There's an opening inside!

She walked through the front door and saw a small line at a weird thing that the workers were typing on. After they typed, numbers and letters would show up on the screen. As one person finished at the thing, the next person stepped up. Victoria walked to the end of the line. She got to the front a few minutes later and said to the attendant, "There was a sign outside that said there was an opening."

"Yes," the attendant said pointing at the baker in the kitchen behind them. "Follow our baker to the back room."

"This way," the baker said, holding the door open for Victoria.

"Coming," Victoria said. As she walked into the kitchen, she shouldered the baker on the way. She couldn't help doing it, because she hadn't done something bad in at least three days.

"Must have been an accident," the attendant muttered to the baker as he closed the door.

The baker and Victoria went to a room in the back. They sat on yellow chairs with pillows in the shape of Bs.

After a few minutes, the interviewer arrived and the baker left. "So, do you have any experience?" asked the interviewer.

"Yes," Victoria said. "I have experience of almost dying and of getting an asteroid that has magic snatched from me."

"I meant job-wise," the interviewer explained and then turned his head.

"Oh," Victoria said. "Then no."

"So this would be your first job?" the interviewer asked.

"Yes," Victoria said. "I need money."

"You want to go shopping?" the interviewer asked.

"Why would I shop?" Victoria asked. "I'm a grown woman."

"Really? You only look 14."

"Exactly," Victoria said.

"But being a '*grown woman*' means you have to be *18*," the interviewer said.

"Well, that's not normal where I'm from," Victoria said, thinking of Mars.

"Back to the interview. By the way, my name is George."

"Okay," Victoria said as she wondered why that was important.

"Are you good at math?"

"Top of my class," Victoria lied, thinking of her math class, and how she got kicked out. But it wasn't her fault that Paisley died because a rock was thrown at her head.

"Good. Do you know how to use a cash register?" George asked.

"Yes," she said thinking back to when she was a person who added up price, operated, and charged the money when she worked at Bob's construction. She didn't want to mention to the interviewer she had no idea what a cash register was. It couldn't be *that* different.

"Can you press certain buttons quickly?" George asked modeling with his fingers.

"Uh-huh," she lied, not knowing what buttons were.

"You're hired," George said stepping up.

"Yes," Victoria *answered*.

"Get to work," George said. "And why did you sound like you were answering a question when I said you were hired?"

"Sorry," Victoria said, hoping her mistake wasn't showing of her being a Martian. "I've never heard the phrase."

"Your uniform is in that closet over there," George said pointing out the door across the hallway.

Victoria got up, walked over to the closet, then took it out. "Can I have some *privacy*?" Victoria said, sounding disgusted.

"Actually, there's a bathroom over there," George said.

"Okay," Victoria replied. She walked out of the room to the door that George pointed at. She went in the bathroom and held out the uniform. She had a black apron, black shirt, and black pants. A green "B" was on the shirt.

She put up her hands, and poof! The uniform magically appeared on her body.

"So I don't even need a job," Victoria said happily "I just need to know which direction to go." Victoria walked out of the bathroom, happy that the orb *actually* worked.

"You'll be working at this cash register," George said. He stood in front of the counter.

"Do you have a map of the Earth?" Victoria asked.

"We have them at the *Knick-Knack Shop*, across the street," George said. "They cost $5."

"Okay," Victoria said trying to remember the name. "Will I get $5 working today?"

"You'll get $7," George said holding a white piece of paper it had a number and a dollar sign on it. It also had a spot to put a name.

"Great," Victoria said walking to the cash register.

"I'll leave it to you," George said. He went outside and took down the sign that had the opening on it.

"I'll take a cheeseburger, a large water, and two children's meals—one with a side of fries, and one with a side of apple slices," said the person in the front of the line.

"Excuse me, who are you?" Victoria asked disgusted, clearly not understanding her job.

"A customer," the customer said.

"Okay," Victoria said now looking at her hands. "So is that what you want?"

"Yes," the customer said.

"Coming right up," she said as she looked curiously at the buttons. She randomly pressed four buttons: a pancake, three children's meals, and no sides.

She watched what the person working at the cash register beside her was doing and pinned the ticket that printed out on the line behind them.

When the baker handed Victoria the order and the receipt, she yelled out the number that was on it like the other cashier. "Number 57!"

The customer with Number 57 walked up and said, "This isn't what I ordered."

"Too bad," Victoria said looking to the other person in line. "Now, go away!"

"Uhh," the customer said, "this person got my-" Poof! The customer was cut off, and she disappeared out of the building. Gone.

"Thanks for the money," Victoria said as she put the money away in the cash register.

* * *

Poof! One more customer gone. Victoria looked out of the window seeing the sun go down. "Almost time," she mumbled to herself.

A few minutes later, after all customers had left, she heard an announcement. "Work's over. Time to leave."

"Yes!" she said as she grabbed $7 out of the register.

She ran to the shop across the street and walked inside. "Are there any maps of the Earth in this shop?" Victoria asked.

"Why of course," said the old lady. She stood behind an old, wooden desk and walked over to show Victoria the maps in the section of the store that said "Globes and Maps."

"So, this is this it?" Victoria asked as she picked up a map that had colorful drawings of something called Asia. Then she saw that there were a lot of other places: Australia, Europe, and then she saw the USA in the map.

"Yep," the old lady said. "That'll be five bucks."

"Here you go," Victoria said as she handed her the money.

"Thanks," the old lady said and walked back behind the counter.

"No," Victoria said thinking of her scheme, "thank *you*."

Victoria left the shop and looked at the map. The beach was just to the side of the road. She noticed the sand.

"So, I'm here, and the USA is over there," Victoria said as she dragged her hand along the map from Western Australia to the Eastern USA. "I guess this is the way to go."

Then she noticed that she was in Eastern Australia. If she went across the Pacific Ocean, she could get there more quickly.

Victoria used her magic to find which way was east.

CHAPTER 13:

SPIES

"Do you want to do *anything?*" Sam asked walking home from school.

"Okay," Sofia said as Sam smiled, "if it has nothing to do with magic."

Sam frowned. "But we *can* do anything," Sam said squinting her eyes. "So why not *do* anything?"

"Because it's dangerous," Sofia said holding her eyes open.

"We haven't gotten caught yet," Sam said making a pink magical fountain come of her hands. Sofia glared at her as if she had stolen her dog. Sam stopped.

"That doesn't mean we won't."

"Please," Sam pleaded leaning her head back in temptation. "Just this once."

"Fine," Sofia said, breaking down. "What do you want to do?" Sofia shrugged.

"How about we travel to the time of the dinosaurs?" Sam suggested now holding up a pink figure of a Tyrannosaurus Rex in her hand.

"What? Are you joking?" Sofia said louder, her face turning red. "We could change what happens in the present. Or even worse, we could get ourselves killed."

"Suit yourself," Sam said. She whipped her hands in the air and swirled into pinkish-purplish mist.

"Sam," Sofia shouted after she left. "Why, why, why?"

* * *

Sam found herself lost in a desert going every which way. The sand was rough, and cactuses popped up everywhere.

"Hello!" Sam shouted to nothing. But a dinosaur.

The dinosaur was incredibly tall, and had a head bigger than its foot. Its arms were as skinny as a pencil, and its teeth were as large as mammoth tusks. But these weren't mammoth tusks.

This ...

was ...

"T-rex!" Sam flung her arms up toward the dinosaur. "What am I gonna do? What am I gonna do? I know! Ahh!" Sam joked to herself.

Roar, roar, roar.

"Why, oh why?"

Sam couldn't feel her hand, let alone use it against the dinosaur. She stood there, not moving, acting like she was waiting for the dinosaur to eat her.

* * *

Sofia waited for Sam to magically pop back onto the sidewalk outside their house. She waited one minute, then asked in her head, *Maybe she's in trouble. I mean, dinosaurs?* "But she has to get out of this herself," Sofia whispered.

* * *

Sam started running.

She couldn't feel her feet, but either way, they wouldn't stop moving. Cactuses were closing in on her, like it wasn't just the dinosaur against her. Her heart was racing as fast as her legs, and her mind was thinking as slow as a sloth. Because her mind wasn't thinking, she didn't see the river running through the long desert. Sam turned just as she saw that she was only a foot away. She couldn't stop.

* * *

Sofia still waited by the steps.

She sat down on the stairs of her house, and she fidgeted by pulling the grass out of the ground. She pulled ... and pulled ... and pulled. Then she stopped. Sofia looked in the direction of the dark alley, on the other side of the street, through the corner of her eye. She thought she saw a boy. A boy who looked alone. But when Sofia turned her head in that direction, the boy wasn't there.

* * *

The boy was panting.

He wasn't supposed to be caught. Once he grabbed his breath out of the "panting mode," as he liked to call it, he went back to looking. He saw Sofia go back to pulling the grass. Then he looked at his ally behind him.

"Did she see you, Mark?" the girl asked looking to the side.

"No. I don't think so," the boy responded quickly looking at Sofia.

"Good," the girl said. Now watching Sofia too. "If you were caught, the Queen would be mad."

"Greta, I wonder why she sent us to look down on Earth," Mark said thinking. "Mars is our home."

"Yeah. Why would she have any business on Earth?" Greta asked looking to the blue sky.

"She said that she wanted to know what happened to the girl who wanted to come here," Mark said pulling out a recording saying that they had to go to Earth and investigate the needs of a visiting girl named Victoria.

"Just curious, I guess," Greta suggested, now focused on Sofia pulling out grass.

Mark wondered about why the Queen was so interested. He thought it over for a long time, and he didn't realize that the time he spent thinking should've been time spent watching. Time was running out for him to find out her plans.

Suddenly, Mark heard Greta whisper, "Okay. I think that she is waiting for her sister to poof back into the yard."

"Huh?" Mark asked, confused by the sudden noise of her sister.

"I said that she's waiting for her sister," Greta repeated pointing at her.

"Oh. Okay," Mark said thinking again.

"But it doesn't really make sense, because everyone knows that Mars is the only planet with a source of magic, let alone magic," Greta said, thinking back to when she was at school back on Mars, "Oh. Did I forget to mention that she's waiting for her sister to poof back?"

"No. There's no source of magic on Earth," Mark said confused again why the topic had changed.

"That's what I said," Greta said opening her eyes wider. "Were you even listening?"

"Maybe. Maybe not."

"Really," Greta said pulling out her version of the recording. "I'm your sister, and right now, I'm the boss of you."

"So," Mark said pulling his shoulders up, "that doesn't mean I *always* have to listen to you."

"I'm the eldest, though," Greta said. She puffed her chest out a little more. "I will be in charge of making the invisibility spell over Mars, to protect us from the humans' confusing machines."

"Yeah, yeah," Mark said waving his hand down. "Just like Mom and Dad do."

"Mark, that's a really important job," Greta said putting her hand on his shoulder.

"Greta, I don't care," Mark said in the same way, yet somehow more annoying.

"Whatever," Greta said pulling her hand to her face.

"Can you hear me?" said a voice out of the contact speaker in Greta's hand. "It's the Queen."

"Yes," the two said concerned about why the Queen was calling them right now.

"Have you found the girl I described?" the Queen asked calmly.

"We found the girl a while ago in Australia, Now we followed the magic to America," Greta said professionally. "We're looking at the people she's after."

"Who are they?" the Queen asked.

"They seem to either be good friends or sisters, from the way they act toward each other," Mark reported.

"What would she want with them?" the Queen asked.

"Sofia said that she was waiting for her sister to pop back onto the lawn," Greta said.

"Oh, magic," the Queen said. "She wants to get rid of magic. Now I get it. She wants Earth to be saved from magic and to save those girls from being attacked by magic."

"You are smart, my Queen," Greta said.

"Yes, I am," the Queen said. "But she isn't. She doesn't know that you can't vanish magic into nothingness. You have to either absorb it or kill the person with magic."

"So, do you have the information you need?" Mark asked.

"Yes," the Queen said.

"Well, I have a suggestion," Greta said. "She probably doesn't even know that the girls have absorbed it. She's in a distant land called Australia."

"Is that far?" the Queen asked.

"I said distant," Greta said.

"What would she be trying to do?" the Queen said.

"Maybe she wants to absorb the magic," Mark suggested.

"Don't be stupid, Mark," Greta said. "That's a — "

"Great idea," the Queen said.

"It is?" Greta *and* Mark said.

"It is," the Queen said. "I knew she was a bit ambitious. But I didn't think that she was this ambitious."

"Oh. I thought that she was this good person who was treated badly because of how ugly she *looked*," Greta said.

"Apparently not," Mark said. "Looks evil, is evil."

"Couldn't have said it better myself," the Queen said, "which is why she is a threat. She is going to absorb the powers and defeat me. We can't have that."

"The only way to stop that would be to either kill Victoria or kill the two girls," Greta said.

"Exactly," the Queen said gruesomely.

"So you want us to *kill?*" Greta asked.

"Fun," Mark said.

"No, not fun," Greta said nervously.

"Oh, yes. Fun," the Queen tried to say convincingly.

Greta turned off the voice teleporter thing, the device that the Queen called a magical version of a walkie talkie.

"We have to kill the twins," Mark said. "Our Queen demanded."

"We can't," Greta opposed.

"Yes, we can," Mark disagreed.

"It won't be good," Greta pointed out.

"Yes, it will," Mark said. He smiled.

"I'll speak your language," Greta explained. "It won't be *fun.*"

"Yes, it will," Mark disagreed, smirking.

"You just like disagreeing with me, don't you?" Greta asked, annoyed.

"Yes, but that's just a bonus," Mark said.

"So you want to kill them?" Greta asked.

"I do," Mark answered. "I have to follow my Queen's orders."

"It's your choice," Greta said.

"Yes," Mark said. He turned back around.

"You can pick," Greta added.

"Uh-huh," Mark said. His eyes opened wider as he looked at Greta.

"Any option you want."

"I picked yes," said Mark, annoyed.

"Okay, if that's what you want," Greta said. "But do we have to?"

"We don't *have* to, but we should," Mark said. "Our Queen has power over us, and we can't exactly face her *entire* army."

"Oh. You're scared of her army," Greta said. "Well, don't be. We don't have to go back to Mars."

"We should," Mark said. "Is it easy to breathe here to you?"

"No," Greta admitted, "but that doesn't mean we have to go back. We can find a way."

"I don't think it's as easy as that," Mark said.

"But what if it is?" Greta asked.

"Saying you can do something and actually doing it are two *completely* different things," Mark said.

"That doesn't –" Greta stopped herself. "It seems impossible now, but –"

"See, you can't fight it," Mark interrupted. "You know we have to do this. We have no other option."

"Fine," Greta said. "But first, how are we going to kill them?"

"I saw a sign in front of a store called the Army Shop," Mark said. "It said something like this:"

Get Your Weapons Here

And Be Prepared For The

Next World War

"Do you think it's the kind of army we have on Mars?" Greta asked. "Like when the army uses their weapons to make the people who steal go to the Queen's dungeons, then they get killed on the first day of the next month?"

"Maybe," Mark said, "but this place seems pretty strange. So we should go check it out, but let's not get our hopes up."

"Okay," Greta said. "Which way?"

"That way," Mark said. His hands were in the air and pointing to his right.

CHAPTER 14:

FAIRIES

Victoria held up the map to the sky. She didn't notice how the beautiful sunset colors were bleeding through the paper.

"Take me to where what I desire the most lies," Victoria said. She turned to finish the incantation toward the ocean. "With a little army at my side."

A magical voice crept into her mind. "The magic that you own is not strong enough. Your army will be fairies, and your place is here."

"Fairies? And staying? Really?" Victoria said, frustrated. "Well they're in for a ride, being with me."

A line of black mystical magic floated through the sky. It ran into a blob of pink magic and crushed it into little pieces. The pieces grew into large figures. They were fairies. They had wings, they could shrink, and pixie dust followed them. These figures had everything a fairy has.

"Hey," a peeping little voice cried out, "I was just about to buy a pixie cake from a cart driving down the street."

"Yeah? You're my army now," Victoria said. "I used my magic to gather a couple of the fairies. I think it selected the worthiest few. You should be honored."

"I guess so," the fairy said. "My name is Elizabeth."

"My name is Ellie," said the green-clothed fairy.

"My name is Sean," a fairy wearing a football jersey that was way too big said.

"And my name is Catalina," said the fairy with purple clothes.

"So you're my army?" Victoria asked, disgusted.

"Don't act so surprised," Ellie said. "I am *very* powerful. Whose pixie dust was it when I flew to the other side of the galaxy?"

"And I'm not in galaxies, but I'm an A-plus student in Magical Education," Catalina said. "I think dark thoughts, too. Here's an example: I can banish you to an inescapable place, where there is total, endless misery."

"Okay," Victoria said, scared.

"And I have been on the football team at my school for a long time," Sean said. "Long enough that I learned a lot offense moves that are probably powerful enough to use in the real world. Officially called impressive."

"I'm not famous, not good at school, and not on a sports team," Elizabeth said. "So I don't know why I'm here."

"You are useless," Victoria said, disgusted. "A miserable waste of magic. You are an invisible flake of nothing."

"Why are you so mean?" Elizabeth shouted. She held out her hands, and a wave of blue magic came out and blasted Victoria far into the ocean.

"Oh. So you're here because your emotions can destroy anything," Catalina said.

"It seems so," Victoria said as she popped back onto the beach. "Can we start going? Oh I didn't tell you! I am searching for magic that's from Mars."

"No," Catalina said. "We need to wait for the magic to be used before we can locate it."

"Why?" Ellie asked, looking at Catalina.

"We can't track it if there's no recent signature of it," Catalina answered. "So now we wait."

"But it can only be used if it is in someone's soul," Victoria said, using her knowledge of magic.

"Not really," Catalina said. "It has a mind of its own. All magic does. So, let's just wait."

CHAPTER 15:

A TERRIBLE SECRET

Sofia sat in her room and tried to read a book she'd checked out from the library.

Sofia thought about what had happened an hour ago. How could Sam be in dinosaur time and still make it home in time for dinner? Sofia put her book down after she finished the 18th chapter.

Sofia walked down the stairs to her front yard. She saw two people. Sofia looked at them closely and saw them running down the street behind the tree overledge. She followed them down the street.

Ninth Street was busy with all the tourist stores. They stopped, and Sofia heard the girl say, "This looks like the weapon store."

Sofia wondered why they needed a weapon. She walked in the store behind them. Guns stacked the walls and glass counters. Sofia and the two other people hid behind the counters when a salesman walked by. Sofia saw the other two people, but they didn't seem to see her.

She heard the boy whisper, "So, we're really doing this? We're killing Sam and Sofia?"

"We have to," the girl said.

When Sofia heard what they said, she got scared, and she panicked. She walked out of the store and waited for the two to come outside. When they walked out a few minutes later, a gun-shaped bulge was beneath the boy's shirt. Sofia walked up behind them. She put out her hands gently. They must have sensed something, because they looked back at Sofia. Her hands changed into invisible lasers and zapped the two. They fell to the ground. Sofia knew they were dead.

Sofia teleported the bodies to somewhere in New Zealand, then ran back home. She regretted the decision she had made, but they would've killed her. It was an ongoing war between common sense and her hopes for her sibling and her own life.

As Sofia approached her house, she realized it didn't matter whether she should have done it or not. The only thing that mattered was that she killed them. She killed two innocent people. She killed.

CHAPTER 16:

ATTACK THE PAST

Sam flopped around in the river, trying to get out. She tried to calm down, knowing it wouldn't help her get out if she was stressed out about the water. It was only maybe seven feet deep, but with the current it didn't matter.

Sam calmed down and tried to find out which way was up. She swam in one direction. She hit the river floor.

Sam was tired. Her legs wouldn't move. She thought that she should sit on the rock next to her on the river floor.

She was torn between the urge of the water and the value of her life. *If you go down, you won't get up. But it's so comfy. I guess I could stay a little while. No! Move!*

Sam got up and moved in the other direction. Finally, her faced dripped with water as she inhaled a giant breath.

The T-Rex was a few feet away, drinking from the river.

Sam crept quietly away from the T-Rex. But suddenly, a cracking sound filled the silence. The T-Rex turned toward her.

Sam repeatedly pulled her hand down, but nothing happened.

* * *

Sofia felt a tingling in her hands. It got stronger ... and stronger ... and stronger. "What's going on?" Sofia exclaimed. Her whole body was shaking. She couldn't take it anymore. Sofia pointed her finger into the sky and twirled it, creating a pinkish-purplish vortex.

* * *

Sam was about to accept her fate. *You were right, Sofia. I shouldn't have overused my magic.*

The T-Rex was closing in on her. An orange rock was behind her, and the T-Rex was coming.

Sam had lost all hope. But then a swirl of pinkish-purplish magic appeared in the endless desert.

"Sofia!" Sam shouted. "Help!"

"I'm coming!" Sofia shouted back. Sofia held out her hands toward the T-Rex, and a loud ringing noise sounded in the air.

The dinosaur turned around and faced Sofia. "Hey, monster. Guess what happens to people who mess with my sister?" Sofia shouted. A beam of white magic burst out of Sofia's hands and knocked off the dinosaur's arm. "Not good things," Sofia said.

Sofia ran into the explosive red blood toward Sam as the dinosaur rushed away.

* * *

Meanwhile, at the Natural History Museum in Washington D.C., the T-rex bones in the dinosaur exhibit lost an arm.

* * *

"Sam are you okay?" Sofia asked.

"I'm fine," Sam said. "Just ... stunned."

"Okay. Let's get home," Sofia said. She pointed to the sky and twirled her finger again. They disappeared into the pinkish-purplish vortex.

* * *

In Miami, the shadows began to get darker. A black line of magic appeared and landed outside the home of Sam and Sofia.

"Looks like this is the place," said a dark figure. "Now I have to get to the asteroid."

CHAPTER 17:

WE FOUND THE MAGIC

Catalina ran across the beach to where everyone else was sleeping.

"Guys!" Catalina exclaimed. "We found the magic. It was used somewhere in a place called Florida."

"Seriously?" Victoria groaned as she awoke.

"Let's go," Catalina said. Ellie cast a spell that routed a path across the ocean in the east. They all started flying and were off to the magic.

* * *

Victoria and her group were led to a store in Miami on Ninth Street.

"The magic must have moved," Catalina said, as she noticed nothing magical. "We'll follow its trail." Victoria led them through town, and they ended up near a house. They sat down in the bushes. Victoria looked through the window and saw three people: a man with brown hair and a salt-and-pepper beard and two gorgeous young girls who looked exactly alike.

While the man was in the kitchen, one of the girls floated a pepper shaker in her direction.

"This is going to be a little harder than we thought," Victoria said. "It looks like the magic is already attached to a soul. We'll have to find some way to get the magic out."

"So what are we going to do?" Catalina asked still looking to the girls.

"We should make camp somewhere and mix potions or something to find out what can take their powers," Victoria said.

"There's a dark alley over there," Elizabeth suggested.

"Okay," Victoria said. "We'll have to put up a protection spell. Catalina, create some sleeping bags and forge an invisible portal to that miserable world I created just for you."

"Gladly," Catalina said, as she pointed her fingers toward the alley. Sleeping bags appeared. Then they disappeared.

"Where'd the sleeping bags go?" Elizabeth asked. "Did you make them invisible to me? Do you hate me that much?" Elizabeth's voice got louder. A blue wave of magic appeared and blasted Catalina into the alley, where she disappeared.

Catalina walked out of the alley and said, "You're lucky I landed on a sleeping bag. Come in."

CHAPTER 18 :

LET'S MAKE A PLAN

"Good morning," Sean said. "Just like in football, we need to make a plan, before they do."

"We could find out their weaknesses and use those against them," Victoria suggested.

"I was thinking something more like thinking of what to do to ask them for the magic," Sean said. "To, you know, be fair."

"I like my idea better," Victoria said tilting her head in fake thought.

They walked up to the glass window to get a view of them. They saw the same old-looking man sitting at a desk and typing on a computer.

"That's the guy we saw last night," Catalina said.

"Yeah," said Elizabeth. "Maybe he's their Dad."

"Probably," Victoria said, "but he's not the person who has magic."

"So what are we supposed to do? Wait 'til the girl comes back?" Sean asked.

"I guess so," Victoria said. She sat in a bush. "We need to hide."

* * *

Later that night, Victoria's army of fairies were itching, literally, to get out of the bushes.

"This is so uncomfortable," Elizabeth said. "Do the thorns hate me? I did nothing. I shouldn't be scratched. I didn't do a thing. Why are you trying to do this? I feel horrible. Why do you treat me this way? I did nothing." Elizabeth shouted, and a wave of blue magic splashed out of her hands. The bush disappeared into thin air.

Pop!

"Get into my bush and don't feel offended," Catalina said. She used her hands to create a new bush.

Suddenly a soft voice came from around the corner of the block. "Sam, what did you get on your math test?"

"Why are we talking about such stupid things, when you and I both know that we have to tell somebody that we both have magic?" a second girl said in an upset voice.

"Well, it looks like the magic is in two," Sean said looking up at Victoria with a smirk on his face.

"Yay! We have to find the weaknesses of *two* people," Victoria said looking Sean straight in the eye with excitement and her annoyed nature shining through.

"Still don't agree with that, but who cares? What Sean thinks doesn't matter," Sean said. He looked at Victoria in a "really?" kind of way with a high pitched voice.

"Shut up, Sean. They're coming," Victoria whispered holding a finger over her mouth as the girls slowly walked up to the porch, with a palm tree giving them shade.

They all shuffled to the back of the bushes and waited silently. Catalina was casting a spell to block them from hearing the shuffling in the bushes.

"You know, Sofia," Sam said stopping right before the door.

"Know what," Sofia replied itching her eye, which was about to burst from the sun.

"You know that you're way too nice. You think it would be too much of a risk to expose us and get Dad in trouble. You have to realize what's the best for *us*," Sam said pointing to them both.

"Well, I don't think it's worth the risk, unless it's helping someone else," Sofia said pointing to the door as if it was a punishment for someone who had poured water on their head.

Sam opened the door aggressively and flung the keys into the house. The door shut behind them.

"Kindness!" Victoria said jumping up from the suspense, "She's too kind. We have to find some way to exploit that."

"So our plan is to come up with a plan based on exploiting the nice girl's weakness?" Sean said, sounding surprised. "That doesn't sound like a plan. It sounds like a plan for a plan."

"It's a plan!" Victoria shouted. "Now we come up with a plan for the plan."

"Not a plan," Sean whispered into Ellie's ear. "Hey, why have you been so quiet?"

"I wasn't with you until now. I was packing to go home, 'cause I thought this was going to be a bit boring. But then I realized it's like the introduction to movies," Ellie said shaking her head. "And the good part is about to come."

CHAPTER 19:

A GREAT COINCIDENCE

"What do you two want for dinner?" Dad asked Sam and Sofia.

"I want the pasta leftovers from that restaurant we went to, Bella's Italian Café," Sam answered.

"I guess I'll have that too," Sofia agreed.

"Comin' right up," Dad said.

Dad opened the refrigerator and pulled out a white box. He put it on the smooth black counter and opened the box. He opened a cabinet on the wall, pulled out three paper plates, and took a spoon out of the drawer to pick up the pasta and put it on the plates.

"Microwave or oven?" Dad asked.

"I like oven. But I know that takes time, and I'm hungry, so microwave," Sam said in further explanation than needed.

"I don't care," Sofia said focusing on the book she was reading. *"Annie knew the consequences of making the deal. It gave instant bragging rights to everyone at school. She just couldn't let her win the race for the doll she had since she was three. Her dad needed the money that the race winner got. So she yelled "Principal, she stole my favorite doll". The principal came and then he asked for the doll nicely, and then he gave it to her. That was when she was eleven. Now she's seventeen and sitting by her father's death bed..."*

"Microwave it is," Dad said waking Sofia from her book trance.

Dad put the three plates in the microwave and set the timer for one minute.

They waited for the microwave to nuke everything. When it beeped, Dad took the plates out of the microwave and put the food in front of Sam and Sofia.

"Dinner is served," Dad said as he held his hand up in front of his chest like a waiter.

Sam picked up her fork, twirled the pasta around the tines, raised it, and put it in her mouth. "Can I warm up mine a couple more seconds?" Sam asked. "It's a bit cold for my taste."

"Sure," Dad said as he threw away the container that held the food. "And while you're waiting, can you take out the trash?"

"Okay," Sam said. "Twenty seconds."

As Sam walked out of the door with the trash over her shoulder, she heard the annoying buzzing sound of the microwave start. She opened the door and heard someone talking. The sound came from the dark alley across the street. She quietly set down the trash and walked across the street to hear the conversation.

"So, to get the magic out of the girls, we have to kill them?" a voice asked.

"Yes," another voice said. "It won't be tethered to a person. And if you do the right spell in time, you, alone, can absorb the magic."

"And if I don't do the spell?" the first voice asked.

"The magic will dissolve into the air and give everyone a bit more of magic," the second voice replied.

"How long do I have to do the spell?" the first one asked.

"Until its spirit goes to its own afterlife," the second one answered.

"So first, to get her dead, we have to come up with something that puts her kindness against her," said the first voice. "How will we do that?"

"Uhm ... everyone likes dogs. Right?" a third voice said.

"Yeah. We could use a spell that makes dogs explode at a certain time or something," said a fourth voice. This speaker was male.

"Or we could do something less noticeable, like take out its soul and crush it here. Because then the body wouldn't die, just the soul," a fifth voice said. "I don't actually want to kill her, and if we only destroy her soul, then her body will automatically recharge a new blank soul, that we will add her memories and soul back to."

"That's a good plan, except for the keep the body alive part," the first voice said. "Too difficult a spell and not enough magic."

Sam realized she was listening to a group who wanted to kill her sister. She ran back into the house.

"Why were you gone so long?" Dad asked.

"I saw the trash truck leaving, so I made it stop to pick up our trash," Sam lied.

"Okay," Dad said in an 'I'm not listening, but I'm trying to make you think I'm listening' voice.

"Can you come upstairs with me, Sofia?" Sam asked urging her up the stairs.

Sofia finished the paragraph: *"And then Annie ran to her mother's house who had divorced her father. She needed someone to comfort her. She needed someone to comfort her when she lost the race as a child. That's right, she's no longer a child. She is a grown woman. She needed her mom though..."*

"What about your dinner?" Dad asked.

"Not hungry," Sam said.

"Okay," Sofia said, suspiciously. She followed Sam up the stairs and into their room. "What is it?" she asked.

"When I went outside, I saw – well, I heard – these people saying that they want your magic," Sam said.

"Okay. And you believed that?" Sofia asked. "No one knows."

"I just think that we should be a little careful. "They said ... that they will have to kill you to get the magic."

"Okay," Sofia said, a little nervous. "We'll watch out, but I doubt it's true."

"We'll have to see."

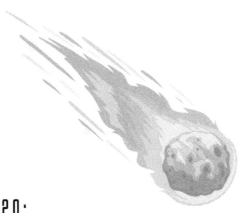

CHAPTER 20:

DOGS

Sam and Sofia were on their way to school the next day.

Sam had her hand on her chin, thinking about what she had heard yesterday.

"Be extra careful," Sam said to Sofia, looking all around as to inspect the area. "But how would they exploit your weakness of being kind?"

"Don't say it that way," Sofia said, shaking her head. "Being kind is a strength."

"Okay," Sam said nodding slowly once, "but that's not how they think."

"So," Sofia said slowly probably out of stress, "we'll have to see if something looks peculiar."

"Is that enough?" Sam asked still looking forward, hoping not to see anything.

"Do we have a choice?" Sofia asked almost pulling her hair.

"I could go back to the alley and find out their exact plan," Sam suggested while holding up a hand, concentrated on getting home with no obstacles.

"Too dangerous."

"Then we don't have a choice." Sam admitted defeat. "But I'll only listen for a minute."

"You're concerned about my safety," Sofia said stopping and grabbing Sam's shoulders. "So that's why you have to understand that I'm worried about *your* safety."

"Okay."

* * *

Sam and Sofia walked the rest of the way to school in silence. They went on with their days a bit distracted from the weekend's discoveries. In each class they were either doodling or looking off into the windows, with a palm tree sticking out of the ground or a bird flying by.

Sam thought, *There's a chance that Sofia might die. I have to do something.*

And Sofia thought, *What if Sam decides to go spy anyway? I have to do something.*

In the end, both of them were yelled at in their classes for not paying attention, and they *still* didn't come up with ideas on what to do.

* * *

Sam and Sofia walked home and found a dog waiting on their doorstep. The dog had golden hair, and the cutest little ears you ever did see. The tail was wagging so much it might have broken.

"Aw," Sofia said as she jogged to the gate, "a dog."

"This might be a trick," Sam said locking the gate temporarily by messing up the numbers on the lock. "What are the chances that a stray dog would randomly be at *our house*, out of all the other doorsteps on this street? On the outskirts of Miami? Where animal control is enforced as if it's murder?"

"We can't just leave him here," Sofia said pointing to the dog. "As you just said, animal control..."

"Actually," Sam said leaning her head from side to side, "yes, we can."

"Really?" Sofia said in a 'that's what you think is best' voice. She bent down to pet it, and the dog started glowing. "What's happening?" she asked frantically.

"I told you someone was after you," Sam said. "Get away!"

Sam and Sofia ran away, and the dog followed them and then soon disappeared. They stopped. "My hand feels funny, and I need to stop," said Sofia shaking her hand harshly. "Ahh!"

A mini dog grew on Sofia's hand. It breathed in, and blue air came out of Sofia's mouth. Sam looked closer and saw the details of Sofia's face on the mini dog. Sofia's body fell to the ground.

"What are you doing, dog!?" Sam screamed immediately going to the ground in shock.

The dog on Sofia's hand and the dog on the ground next to her raced at each other and morphed into five people. Wait, one person. Four things with wings.

"The people from last night?" Sam asked looking to the alley beside them.

"By the way, all we did was take out her soul," said the person, who appeared to be the leader. She shook her black hair and said. "Now we crush it and take her magic." She smiled at a blue ball in her hands. "It's here, inside this blue ball."

"Why would you do this?" Sam asked trying to keep her eyelids shut. Tears came through her eyelids.

"I did this because I want your magic," the leader said nodding quickly. "And because of that, I'm your greatest enemy. Oh, and by the way, my name is Victoria."

Sam sprang at Victoria and took the blue soul out of her hands. Sofia had now been grabbed onto her shirt. She reached for the blue ball in Victoria's hand.

"Sam!" Sofia's spirit said. It was an image of her. But her lips moved. She was just surrounded by blue. Is that how it looks in there?

"Have fun with your last moments," Victoria said looking to the blue ball at first, but then glancing at Sam.

Sofia returned to her body through her mouth, and her body picked itself up.

Victoria and all the people behind her vanished. Or, at least, most of them did.

"Who are you?" Sam asked as she looked at the winged boy in front of her.

"My name is Sean. I don't agree with what Victoria is doing."

"Then what did she mean by last moments?" Sofia asked. She pulled her finger across her neck to show death.

"Victoria had water from the River of Lost Souls on her hands," said Sean taking the bottle out of his pocket.

"You mean from Hades and all that?" Sam asked creating a ghoulish look, and spreading her arms out quite weirdly.

"It's not effective on bodies. But if you put it on a soul, eventually that soul will die from the inside," Sean said now looking at Sofia's sneakers with pink and blue patterns on them.

"How can I fix that?" Sam asked getting lower to get into Sean's sight line.

"You can take out her soul and wash it and stuff, but you need to wash it with a certain potion," Sean said and then tilted his head to the side a little bit.

"And that potion is?" Sofia asked clearly not getting how clueless he was.

"I don't know, but I'm guessing the exact opposite thing. Maybe," Sean said straightening his head.

"Okay," Sam said nodding her head thinking of a solution. "So this is like, we need to find a magical river in Heaven?"

"Yes!" said Sean snapping his fingers. "I gotta go." Sean snapped his fingers again and he was off… somewhere.

"How do you plan to get there?" Sofia asked forcing her eyebrows closer to her eyes.

"I haven't found that out yet," Sam said looking the other way. "Sean? Please?" Sean appeared.

"Sorry. I'm just scared," Sofia said turning around to see Sean.

"It's okay, but how *do* we get to Heaven?" Sam asked as she turned to Sean too.

"I think you have to get close to dying, and then kinda look around and see where it is," Sean suggested. He then lifted his shoulders to his neck.

"And then we can make a portal there," Sam said Spinning around to see Sofia with hope in her eyes.

Sean disappeared in a poof of blue magic, leaving to go back to wherever he was before.

Sofia ran into the house as Sam shouted, "Where are you going?"

Sofia didn't stop. A few minutes later, a figure appeared on top of the house. It was Sofia.

"Sofia, what are you doing up there?" Sam asked knowing exactly what.

"I might die anyway," Sofia said. "I might as well be the one to do this. I trust you. Save me."

"Noo!" Sam screamed beginning to run toward where she would land.

A thousand million bajillion thoughts were going on in her head. But only one mattered. *Save your sister.*

CHAPTER 21:

STAIRWAY TO HEAVEN

Sam filled with panic as she watched Sofia's head fall in front of the rest of her body.

Sam was jittery. She brought up her hand and twisted it up, so Sofia's body went up, then down. Slowly.

Sofia raised up and dipped down to the floor.

"Were you close enough?" Sam asked trying to hide her deep breaths, and stress.

"Kind of," Sofia said holding up her hand, then twisting it side to side. "I saw a large gate. It was white and had curly poles. It was perfect."

"That's enough," Sam said shouting. She hoped not to have to do that again. "We tell our portal to lead us to the most perfect place. Not just in the world, but anywhere."

"It might not work," Sofia shouted down to Sam. "We could be gone a long time and get Dad worried or suspicious."

"Then we'll do it on the weekend."

"Worse. We'll be home then and with him," Sofia said cuffing her hands around her mouth now.

"We'll say we're on a weekend-long sleepover," Sam replied.

"Won't Dad want to communicate with us?" Sofia asked. "I don't think there's cell service in Heaven."

"Magic!" Sam shouted up to Sofia. She wondered if magic could create cell service. If so all problems in the world would be solved. "We use magic."

"Isn't that what got us into this whole mess?" Sofia asked looking darker with the sun behind her.

"Yeah," Sam said nodding her head and becoming higher pitched. "So it's magic's job to get us out of it."

"I don't think that's how it works," Sofia shouted moving her eyes right to left.

"Well, what you think is your opinion," Sam said her voice drifting off. Her voice came back abruptly, "And if you keep your opinion, you die!"

"Okay, fine. We'll do it," Sofia said chuckling.

"So come up with a spell to transfer the memory," Sam said pointing to Sofia then herself.

"Okay." Sofia paused forcing her eyeballs up.

"Got it," Sam said opening her eyes, which she had just found out were closed.

"You ready to ... die?"

"I guess so," Sofia said tilting her head to the left.

Sam and Sofia opened a portal that led to bright yellowish-white light awning for them to come through. Sam and Sofia jumped through the portal, Sofia from the roof, and everything got brighter. Behind them, the portal disappeared so it looked like the light endlessly surrounded them. Then they zoomed forward and fell to the ground, covered in grass. White pearly gates curved along the ground. It was perfect, as Sofia described.

"This is it," Sam said.

"So, do we just walk in?" Sofia asked.

"No," Sam replied, "I think that God comes to visit us and greet us to welcome us to Heaven. Do you remember if a misty figure came over the gates?"

"Yeah, but that was when I was actually *dying*," Sofia said. "I think we have to sneak in before he sees us and sends us back."

"Where exactly is the opening?" Sam asked.

"I think it's anywhere," Sofia said as she stepped up to the gate. The gate's curves faded away so the two could get through.

Sam walked through and found herself in a perfect place with misty figures crowded everywhere. Everyone was smiling. To Sofia it smelled like her grandma's perfume, but to Sam, it had smelled like strong cinnamon. They both just realized that all their scrapes and cuts had disappeared.

They walked quickly through the crowds and passed all types of people, just like in the living world. Jocks. Fashion fiends. Artists. All of whom had a unique clothing style.

"This is so weird," Sam whispered to Sofia, looking at a jester who was standing on two tennis balls, juggling eight bowling balls, with a parrot on their head, not to mention the auto-applause machine.

"Just focus on finding the river," Sofia whispered pointing straight forward.

"How are we supposed to find it if we can't talk to anybody?" Sam asked looking around at all the people.

"Maybe there's like a map somewhere," Sofia suggested looking around the town.

"Or we could find something like a community map?" Sam asked now looking too.

"Good idea," Sofia said as she looked around the other way and saw a large, rounded sign across the street.

Sam and Sofia walked across the street, and one of the misty figures walked directly through Sofia. "What?" Sofia asked. She looked back at the woman who had walked through her.

"I think it's like how we can walk through ghosts and we don't see them," Sam said. "We're ghosts here, so no one sees us."

"Cool," Sofia said as she walked straight through someone for fun.

Sam and Sofia continued their walk and got to Main Street.

"So, we are here," Sofia said as she pointed to Main Street, "and we need to get here." She pointed to Star Stream, the river in Heaven that is said to heal anything with its waters.

"So, we have to go this way," Sam pointed to the right.

Sam and Sofia walked through the crowds of people until Main Street turned into a street with crowds of houses. Then it became a dirt road. Then it became a meadow.

In that meadow was a little shack beside a river. Shining stars floated on the low waves.

"Are you ready?" Sam asked looking to Sofia in nervousness. "This might hurt a little."

"Yes," Sofia said. She stood a little straighter and opened her mouth.

Sam brought out her hand and waved it over Sofia. Her sister's eyes went white, and her mouth fell open wider. A floating white spirit came out of her mouth. Blackness had begun to attack across the spirit's legs, and Sofia fell to the ground. Sam stared at Sofia's motionless body. Then she walked over to the stream, cupped her hands, and lowered them to the water. As soon as she was an inch away, she flew backward and hit a tree behind her. At least there was no pain there.

"What the heck?" Sam asked as she rubbed her head, then realized there was no point.

An old lady walked out of the small wooden shack at the side of the river. Her face had what looked like long sewing marks over her eyes. These stitches blinded her from the world.

"Who are you?" Sam asked as she walked closer to the figure. "Oh, right. You can't see me. Ugh. Now I can't get the water, because you will be too confused."

"Actually, I can sense you there," the woman said.

"How? You don't even have eyes."

"I'm Ella the Seer," the old woman said. "I see the future, but I don't have eyes. That's the funny thing about us. We can see everything but what's right in front of us."

"So how do you see me then?" Sam asked.

"You're not actually here. Only the spirit of you in a body form," Ella said. "You are really on the sidewalk, sprawled and lifeless. Because I can see the future, I knew that someone who was not dead would come here one day."

"Well, can you help me?" Sam asked, pointing to the river. "It has a protection spell—"

"On it," Ella finished. "Sorry. I see the future. Why do you need to have water from the Stream of Stars?" Ella asked.

"It's the only thing that can save my sister's soul," Sam said. "She was poisoned from the River of Lost Souls."

"Well, the Stream of Stars isn't the cure for that." Ella said this like it was the most obvious thing in the world. "You just need a very good medicine. See, the River of Lost Souls here in Heaven has become like the flu. Because nowadays, lots of people don't follow the rules, and are pushed into a portal to the underworld, where they are shortly punished by Hades."

"Do you have that medicine? If so can I have some?" Sam asked with her hands crossed together.

"Not unless you have something to offer me."

"Anything, anything," Sam pleaded about to fall on the ground. "I want to save my sister."

"Well, you see I have been cursed and if you think that I am a good person, the curse will be broken," Ella said.

"What is your curse?" Sam asked.

"Once I was a little girl, in a little town, in a little country, in the littlest region of Europe. I had a sister. She was sick with a mental illness and tried to destroy everything. Everything. One day I came to my home with a mate. I had fallen in love. My sister, with her mental illness, suggested she wanted to destroy my mate. One night when my mate was coming by so we could go out to get porridge, my sister came into the room. She was quite young at that point, and my mate thought she was adorable. He went to talk with her, and she saw her chance to get rid of him. She took him down to the ground by pulling on his leg, until he tripped, and he lay there, defenseless. She punched, and punched, and punched. His lip busted open. Back in my days, that was serious. As he went out the door, my sister tripped him, and he fell again. The rip in his lips became infected, and a few days later he died." Tears came through the stitches on her eyes as Ella told her story.

"That's horrible," Sam said. She was sorry that Ella had lost her true love.

"I went into her room that next night and I – I – I – I killed her. Her blood spattered into my eyes, and I was blind for a small moment. But after I washed my face, I still couldn't see. I was blind, then, and guilty. I was accused of murder, and I was hanged. Before I died, though, my blindness left for half a second or less. It was enough to see my parents crying. After I died and came here, I was cursed to not see anything but the future. And only in flashes. It tormented me. I felt like the world was toppling down on me. One day, when I was sure my parents were here, I went across the meadow to see them. I had not left the meadow before, because I was still haunted by the visions, and more people means more thoughts of their future, because I see their future when I'm around people naturally, and love mates' future, and relatives' future, and it starts a stress attack. I tried to leave but I couldn't. Every time I left this meadow, a big poof of magic sent me back. My curse is that I can't leave this small, small, meadow."

"How are we supposed to help you?" Sam asked.

"You are the prophesized ones," Ella said in a grand tone. "You are destined to have powers. Powerful ones."

"Yep, we remember. Those aren't new," Sofia said. She waved her hands, and sparks flew from them.

"You are either destined to be the most valiant heroes and defeat the strongest evil in the lands, or else be the strongest evildoers and defeat the most valiant heroes in the lands."

"Wow. Big difference, right?" Sam said looking at her hand hoping to never become an evildoer. "So, what do we need to do to, you know, help?"

"You see, all you need to do is see me for the person I am and not for the person I was in life," Ella said. "A good person."

"Then why did you tell us the story?" Sam asked, as she walked through the door of the small hut. "Oh, wow!"

The hut was not a hut. Or, at least from the inside, it wasn't. When they walked inside, they entered a huge room much bigger than the outside portrayed. It was like an apartment, but old-timey, with much more space. The problem was, the whole room was on fire. The bed, the icebox, the small table, the hardwood floors, even the water on the counter.

As Sam looked around the room, she heard a slight buzzing. She thought it was Ella answering her question.

"I should put Sofia's soul back," Sam said, and then floated Sofia there, and forced it into her.

"Can you repeat that?" Sofia asked, clearly being able to remember the conversation, even when her soul wasn't in.

"It's the way to stop loopholes. The believing doesn't work without the story. If I didn't tell the story, you would be put under a curse called hatred's eye, a curse that makes you suddenly start to hate me," Ella finished, her mouth curving to show dismay.

They walked through the house and stopped at the small table. The seer sat down on the single chair. The weird thing was, she didn't burn or even flinch when she touched the flames.

"Um ... you do realize that you are sitting in an on-fire chair, right?" Sam asked. She felt weirded out.

"Oh? Well, you don't really notice if it doesn't hurt, and you have your eyes stitched together," Ella said calmly.

"Okay. Well, give us a reason to believe in you," Sofia said.

"I have changed," the seer said.

"Well then," Sam said, "help us reach the river."

"I can't do that," Ella said.

"Okay," Sofia said. "We have to leave."

"I thought you were the nice one," Ella said flatly, probably able to tell the future.

"Not when it's her life at stake," Sam explained tilting her head, tears almost bursting through.

"Oh," Ella said remembering the conversation from the future.

"Now will you help?" Sofia asked stepping closer.

"I can't do it," Ella said. "I literally can't."

"Can't, or won't?" Sam said as she started to stomp out, then went back in so she could here the answer that could save her sister's life.

CHAPTER 22:

PLAN B

Where are they? Victoria asked herself as she waited.

"I don't see them," Catalina replied glancing in different rooms of the house.

"I wasn't asking you," Victoria said staring at her with weak eyes. "How did you read my mind?"

"The poison shouldn't have killed Sofia yet," Catalina said looking the other way, completely changing the subject. "They must have a way to stop the wretched soul from dying, or they would be here ready to mourn the loss."

"Then we need a Plan B," Victoria said looking up at the pink room, that they figured was the girls'. "But what?"

Catalina and Victoria were hiding and thinking in the bushes of the twins' house. Birds flew through the wind. Trees swayed from the breeze. Then, everything went still. There was no more breeze. The birds were quiet.

"I think we should, like, try to threaten them somehow," Catalina said holding a fist up, where Victoria can't see.

"Not evolved enough," Victoria said, putting her fingers to her chin. "Remember, they're more powerful than we are."

They sat in silence for a few minutes. Victoria saw a dog fight. One dog, two dogs, three dogs. The first dog was about to jump on the third dog. The second dog got in the way, and instead the first dog landed on the second. Then the dogs seemed to get along, and Victoria thought, *out of threat and conflict*. All three walked away. None of them flinched, but she saw fear in the eyes of the second and third dogs.

"I've got it!" Victoria exclaimed recalling the confusing incident of the dogs.

* * *

Later that night, Victoria and Sean stood outside of the twins' house. They walked up to the door. Sean knocked on it, with a galaxy colored hat in his hand.

"Computer delivery," Sean said in a deep voice. He whispered, "I saw a shop that said Personal Computers."

"Works," Victoria whispered.

She heard Dad mutter angrily, "Must be for the girls," as he opened the door.

Victoria grabbed the galaxy-looking hat from Sean, and raised it to the door, about six feet off the ground. Dad asked, "What type of com—"

Dad was cut off as he was thrust into the endless hat.

"Got him," Victoria said. A smile appeared on her face.

"Our plan is going exactly the way you want it," Sean said putting his fingers together, the way that cheesy villains do. "Mwahahahah—"

"Not funny," Victoria said putting a hand over his mouth.

Sean and Victoria walked into the alley and disappeared where the tent should be.

"We have our hostage," Victoria said holding up the hat as if it was a piece of treasure.

* * *

Victoria walked into a dark room. When she opened the door, a red light came on.

"Where am I?" Dad asked tired and hurt.

"Up your butt and around the corner," Victoria said sarcastically tilting her head. "Welcome to Mars."

CHAPTER 23:

COMING BACK

"Fine. I can help you reach the river," said Ella the seer looking down.

"But ..." Sam said nodding slowly, seeing the reluctance in her face.

"It would cost me," Ella said now looking at them. "My mate that I mentioned, he will leave Heaven."

"Why?" Sofia asked putting a hand on her shoulder.

"The river is a way to leave this place. The water can cure anything. So if I help anyone reach the river, or I reach the river, he leaves. That way, I'm not tempted to leave this miserable field of emptiness."

"Please," Sofia pleaded with her hands intertwined, "I don't think Heaven would do that."

"Are you kidding?" Ella said turning around because tears were sneaking through the stitches again. "Heaven was only made to make bad people jealous. The underworld was created by Heaven. All of this happened because a spirit wanted *bad* people to get what *they* deserve, not what *we* deserve."

"Oh," Sofia said blankly looking down at the grass. She thought back to all the things her parents had told her about Heaven and realized none of it is with good intentions. It's too bad. She was excited to come here one day, now that it's certain that it's true.

"I didn't know," Sam said looking at the seer.

"Of course, you didn't," the old seer said. "No one does."

"Then how do you know it's true?"

"They told me," Ella said bringing up her hands her head drooping down. "They tell everyone who goes to a bad place."

They stood in silence for over five minutes. Neither knew what to say. They didn't want to be rude, but they wanted to save themselves.

Then Ella said, "Fine. I'll do it. You're young, and he's over 1,000 years old. Besides, it might get me closer to leaving this meadow."

"But your love?" Sofia said with half of her blonde beautiful hair covering her face. It got there because she repeatedly looked down and tilted her head to cover her tears.

"But you?" the seer said, bringing her hands out to them.

"Okay," Sofia said. Tears of empathy were in her eyes. "So how?"

Ella was halfway across the flaming room.

* * *

The old seer lifted her hands to the cloudless sky. Even though her eyes were sewn shut, she seemed to look at something.

"Um ..." Sam said looking to the seer wearing brown clothes as if she was a seer. "What are you doing?"

"I'm opening the barrier to the river," Ella said. She pointed her hands down toward the perfectly green grassy hill.

A white shield-shaped object appeared. Starting at the top, it slowly disappeared.

Ella stepped through the spot where the shield had come down. "I'm free!" she exclaimed. "But he isn't," Ella said quietly, looking down.

Suddenly, a hologram image appeared in the river. "Hello Ella," the hologram said calmly. "We have seen your improvement. You helped these girls over your mate, even though you only knew them for one day. So, we have decided to let your mate live. And unstitch your eyes. And uncurse you from seeing the future." The hologram had honey-dark skin and long, straight hair. Her eyes were the color of leaves in late summer, her hair was the color of midnight black. She wore a beautiful blue dress with stars as clear as a night on the countryside.

Ella stood still, drawn to what the hologram might say next. "I didn't see this coming in my visions," Ella said curiously.

"We couldn't let you," the beautiful girl said. She swayed her arms. "If we let you see what might happen, you wouldn't become the person you are. You needed to feel hopeless, so that you could tell them you would destroy the border."

"So, can I be with my mate?" Ella asked, her posture straighter, her eyes wider, her feet on toes...

"You mean, your husband?" the hologram asked. She flicked her fingers, and a cart appeared. Ella was in it now, but her eyes were unstitched, and the grief was off the corner of her lips. A handsome blond-haired boy in a tuxedo sat next to her. Ella's eyes were a deep shade of blue so beautiful that someone could sink in that sea after staring for half a second.

"Jonathan!" Ella yelled, and she hugged the boy next to her. "Thank you."

"No, I am not the one to thank," the hologram said with a smile. "You went through this journey by yourself."

The happily now-married couple waved and rode away on the cart. They followed a path along the side of the winding river. The hologram disappeared at the same time Ella and her husband were lost in the distance.

Awestruck, Sam and Sofia stood in the field next to the mystical river.

"Now for you," Sam said. She stepped toward Sofia and put her hand near her mouth, then grabbed her soul. "If medicine will work, this river will do okay right?" Sofia's soul was black everywhere except the center. Her heart. The most human part of herself.

"Uh-oh," Sam said nervously. Sofia's eyes were white as she dropped to the ground.

"Okay. So, I, like, dip it in?" Sam asked out loud. She slowly dipped Sofia's soul in the waters. As soon as a tiny part of it hit the water, it turned back to the beautiful Sofia in a blue ball Sam knew and loved again. Sam pulled her out of the water.

"Sam," Sofia's soul said. She was relieved and had a lighter grip on the soul.

"I'm gonna get you back in," Sam said as she nodded. Sam grabbed Sofia's hand and went right through it. "Right," Sam said. She grabbed Sofia's neck using the magic she needed and put the soul back in Sofia's body.

Sofia's eyes opened to the sky so blue that she could fall up inside of it and never come down. "I feel so much better," Sofia said shaking her hands. She went in for a hug, and their long blonde hair swayed in the wind. "More free." Sofia laughed.

"Sofia!" Sam exclaimed, relieved to have her in better condition.

"Let's go home," Sofia said, detaching from Sam's strong grip.

"I strongly agree," Sam said merrily.

Both thought of memories of standing outside of their front yard. A portal appeared, and Sam said, "Let's go home." Sam and Sofia walked through.

* * *

"Dad!" Sofia and Sam exclaimed as they walked through the front door to see the familiar kitchen.

"Dad?" Sofia asked as she went through the living room.

"Dad?" Both asked as they searched through the whole house.

"I didn't see him," Sam said looking at Sofia with a little worry.

"Me neither," Sofia said. They went inside their room.

"Where could he be?" Sam asked bringing out her cell phone to find Dad.

"I don't know," Sofia said getting her phone out too. One of the rarest occasions she would take her phone out.

"He doesn't have anything planned, right?" Sam asked pulling up his contacts.

Sofia had already looked through his planner. "Nothing."

"Where could he be?" Sam asked searching for 'Dad' in her contacts. She sat on her floral-patterned bed.

A voice came out of the ceiling. "Hello, Sam and Sofia."

CHAPTER 24:

PLAN B ACTIVATION

"So, what are you going to do with me?" Dad asked. He was hanging from a rope tied to his arms a few yards off the ground.

"Oh, you?" Victoria asked looking back to him as if she forgot he was there, which she probably did. "You're bait to get your daughters."

"Why do you want my daughters?" Dad asked trying to look at them, but he was facing the other way.

"They haven't told you?" Ellie asked coming back around to see Dad's face. "Oh. Well, they have magical powers that I would like to steal."

"You mean, I would like to steal, don't you?" Victoria asked Ellie as if she had just killed someone.

"Oh, yes," Ellie said quickly, before stepping away. "Sorry."

"Well, you know what?" Victoria said turning around to where she saw her, with eyes squinting like she was in a sand storm. "Sorry isn't cutting it. Catalina, now!"

"Goodbye," Catalina said with a sassy hand coming up to say what she meant 'I really don't like you, and I'm glad your leaving.' As she held out her hands toward Ellie, purple magic burst through her fingers and blasted Ellie far away until she disappeared in the distant plains of rock on Mars. And she didn't disappear because of distance.

"You're not going to do that to me, right?" Elizabeth asked with a hand over her chest like she was offended. She came out of the corner.

"Why not?" Victoria asked hunching her shoulders, then looking at Elizabeth as if she had eaten her dog.

"Pleasure," Catalina said. Once more, she held out her hands. Elizabeth left a shadow on the red floor, and she was blasted until it stopped.

But a few seconds before she disappeared, a giant wave of magic flooded the area. Literally. They had to swim up to be able to breathe. Dad was stuck under the rope tied to him and stayed on the floor of the new pool.

"Should I close it off?" Catalina asked looking at Victoria on the top.

"Sure," Victoria said. Catalina raised her hand and a shield appeared that made the pool seem invisible. Catalina created an island kind of thing made from red crystals. Everyone swam onto it. Or, at least the ones who were left did.

"Get him up here," Victoria said. She pointed to Dad who was under the water probably thinking about what he could've done in his life.

"Okay," Catalina said. She expanded the island, put in the stand covered in ropes and then added Dad, who was still trapped in those ropes.

"By the way," Dad said. He started to catch his breath. "What do you mean by Sam and Sofia have powers?"

Victoria told them the story of how she lived on Mars, how the old leader sent the magical asteroid to this planet, and how she needed it to rule the kingdom.

"Wait," Dad said. "You're doing all this because you want to be the Queen of Mars?"

"Well, I need to," Victoria explained. "I thought I needed it to survive in my town, which along with other towns is extremely poor, and I probably would have died within two weeks. Now I can generate food, so that's not a problem, but now everyone hates me and if I'm not Queen then I still won't survive. Well I guess the Queen likes me, and everyone follows the lead of the Queen. Okay fine I want revenge on Sam and Sofia!"

"From your story, it sounds like thousands of people didn't have enough money. What makes you so special?" Dad asked, proving a point that hadn't yet been made.

"I was the only one willing to do something about it," Victoria said stomping her foot in front of Dad.

"I've seen you use magic, so why do you need my daughters' supposed magic?" Dad asked, defending Sam and Sofia.

"My powers aren't strong enough," Victoria said. "I can't rule Mars."

"Why don't you stay on our planet?" Dad asked curiously. Then he realized the error of his mistake "I mean –"

"That's not a half bad idea," Victoria said looking to Catalina quickly. "New plan! Use the magic we get to take over *his* planet. It is more populous."

"Dang it," Dad said under his breath. He looked up at the sun, then looked down onto Red Crystal Island, as he'd named it. To the side, he saw the beautiful, clear blue water. He waited for his girls to get here.

Dad still couldn't process that his little girls had magic. After all, now he was the one who soothed them when they had nightmares. He made breakfast for them every day and took them to school, too. Did they need him anymore? Now that they have magic, are they the new parents?

"So, I'm gonna need you to speak into this," Catalina said interrupting Dad's thoughts. "Leader's orders." Catalina pointed to a blue thing. It glowed, and a hologram appeared. It was filming Dad. Catalina threw it to Dad, "Say, 'Victoria and her group have captured me. Please free me.' And, filming."

"Uhm, okay," Dad said nervously. "Victoria and her team have captured me. Please come and rescue me." Dad got closer to the blue thing. "Can I tell them I love them?" Dad asked looking to Catalina.

"Sure," Catalina said nodding her head, "it'll make them more compelled to come."

Dad whispered with his hand over it, "I love you, Sam and Sofia. But don't listen to them. It's a trap." Catalina looked at him like he was crazy. It's a hologram!

Catalina took the hologram recorder out of Dad's hands. "That'll be enough of that."

"No. Please," Dad pleaded looking at the hologram recorder still. "Please."

"No," Catalina said. She walked across the island and sat on a crystal chair she had just made.

Dad hung and waited yet again. He was nervous that he was going to die. He was nervous about their plan. It was despicable. He could do nothing about it, and yet in a weird way, he wasn't nervous. Not a bit. Because now, he knew that his little girls, Sam and Sofia, would hear his voice one last time.

CHAPTER 25:

THREE STEPS

"I have your father," the voice on the video continued, sounding like a serious clown.

At first they are serious, and then they laugh. In this case quite harshly.

Sofia waved her hand over it to pause it.

"So," Sam said looking at Sofia, than the hologram thing, "continue."

"Sorry. Just thought you had something to say with that expression on your face." Sofia waved her hand over it again.

"Come to Mars to rescue him, or he dies," the voice said. The camera focused more tightly, and they saw that the speaker was Victoria. "Also, there's going to be a twist, I would say. Your father's waiting."

The camera showed their father. "Uhm, okay," Dad said. "Victoria and her team have captured me. Please come and rescue me." Dad moved closer. "Can I tell them I love them?" Dad asked hopefully.

"Sure," said a voice, "it'll make them more compelled to come."

Dad whispered, "I love you, Sam and Sofia. But don't listen to them. It's a trap."

The video recorder jiggled around, out of focus. A voice said, "That'll be enough of that."

The video ended.

Shocked, the twins sat back on their beds. They were still for minutes. And the minutes felt like hours that felt like days, that felt like years, that felt like torture.

Finally, Sam broke the silence after opening and closing her mouth many times. "How are we going to get to Mars?"

"With our magic," Sofia quickly responded still looking at her hands, which were still like trees' branches in winter, when the snow, wind, and sadness had all blown away.

"That's probably the whole reason she wants us to come. To steal our magic," Sam said, putting a hand to her head like she and Sofia were crazy.

"Well, we have to save Dad," Sofia reasoned now using her hands for emphasis. The snow had fallen off.

"But we can't just give her our magic," Sam said creating a cool mystical curl of pink and blue waves in the air. For a moment there was silence.

"Yeah. But Dad," Sofia said shaking her head as she said Dad. She couldn't believe the thought of her magic being more important than her own father.

"But the rest of whatever she needs the magic to take over." Sam made a point, slapping her hands out of anger on the bed.

"Fine," Sofia said snapping her fingers. It had snowed again.

"Do you know what we're going to do?" Sam asked looking at Sofia now.

"I have no idea," Sofia admitted looking up from her hands.

"We could take it back by force," Sam suggested lifting her shoulders. For the first time they realized that they both had tears coming through their eyes. No one said anything.

"What do you mean, by force?" Sofia asked.

"You know how Victoria got those weird fairy servants? We could get some of our own?" Sam said, ending in a question.

"No," Sofia said looking to the ceiling and back in frustration. "Just no. We would be exactly like Victoria and becoming like her won't help us defeat her."

"Okay," Sam said sarcastically, "You got any ideas?"

Sofia was about to say something when two figures teleported through a portal into their bedroom. They didn't fall to the ground as they should've, however. Because they were fairies.

"What are you doing here?" Sam asked looking at them as the portal disappeared behind them.

"First can we tell you our names?" one asked. Tears came from her eyes. "You are so mean. You are only concerned with why we're here, not about how *we* are feeling, or even bothering to get to know us."

"Okay. Sheesh," Sam said holding her hands up sarcastically like she was backing away from a fairy who had just called her rude for not asking their names, after they teleported very spontaneously to their room. "What are your names?"

"My name is Elizabeth," said the one with tears on her face. She sniffled.

"And mine is Ellie," said the other. Ellie wore dark green and acted bored as she looked at her nails. "And by the way, if you want to know what happened to us, you can just ask."

"Okay," Sofia said. "What happened to you?"

"Well," Elizabeth said with no tears on her face this time, "it's a lo – short story, actually."

"So basically, Victoria shot us through space and time, and we landed in 1652. We lived there until, eventually, the time came to right now," Ellie said like she was saying she had a jacket on when she did.

"Wait. So, how did you stay alive that long?" Sam asked now laying on her stomach on the bed, with her hand supporting her chin.

"Well," Ellie started, nodding, "we kind of lived in Tasiana where no one ever ages."

"Wait," Sofia said. "Taisiana? As in Mary Tase and all that?" Mary Tase is a popular folktale by the way, where a hard-working woman (Mary Tase) gets the job as mayor, and then the former mayor goes to Tasiana to be the mayor of there, and then Mary Tase discovers how badly he is treating everyone, and integrates the people of Earth to Tasiana, which is a Utopia.

"You see, we have this power to travel to different dimensions," Elizabeth said creating a portal that probably leads somewhere. "Including ones that were invented from pure imagination. If someone in any dimension has an idea for a different kind of land, that land *becomes* a real dimension."

"Cool," Sam said. She paused, then said, "Just invented one."

"So anyway, we set a timer to wait for this exact moment," Elizabeth said holding up her phone which said *Timer for 3:27 PM on September 28, 2018 has rung.* "And we came to you to say that we're on your side."

"Why?" Sofia asked looking at the phone.

"*Because,* Victoria shot us through space and time," Ellie said putting the phone away. She tilted her head, like she was saying two plus two is four, "Duh."

"So, what do you want us to do?" Elizabeth asked holding up her posture then relaxing.

"That's what we were just discussing," Sofia said nodded. "So anyway, what I was going to say before you barged in was, could we randomly attack?"

"And then we could steal Dad by sneaking in," Sam said, randomly mentioning ideas.

"And then, *we* could figure out their plan," Elizabeth said nodded as she squinted her eyes.

"Wait. How do you know if you're just finding out *our* plan?" Sam said looking at them as if they have been accused for killing their dog or something.

"Are you accusing me and my partner of lying?" Elizabeth asked soulfully with a hand over her heart. "We would never stoop so low. We only went into Victoria's gang because it was against the laws of magic to not do that. She broke the magical agreement, so now we're free. And I wish everyone who is so mean would just stop!"

And then, everything did stop. The whole world paused. Everyone moving stopped in place. "Whoopsie," Elizabeth said as she raised the spell.

"Okay, we believe you," Sofia said clearly not knowing the world had paused.

"So, our three steps are sneak in, grab your father, and then figure out their plan?" Ellie asked with a knife kind of hand slapping onto her other hand.

"Yes," Sofia said nodded looking to Sam.

Sam walked out the door and said, "Well, let's get going."

CHAPTER 26:

THE INVASION

Sam, Sofia, Ellie, and Elizabeth crept onto Red Crystal Island in their space ship they used to get there.

"This is so annoying." Sam referred to the magical oxygen bubble uncomfortably surrounding the twins.

"Yeah," Sofia agreed putting her hand outside of the oxygen bubble keeping in mind that this was a once in a lifetime opportunity where she could actually feel Mars. Usually it's too cold to go out of the space suit. "You would think with all the magic we have, we could make this thing bigger, so we wouldn't have to stay within two feet of one another."

"Well, if you had read the book that I suggested you read on the ride here, you would know that your powers are weakened here, because you don't have Martian DNA," Ellie said making a magical image of the cover of the book. It said, *The All You Need to Know About Magic Guide to Your New Life.*

"In my defense," Sofia said holding up a finger indicating 'let me explain', "the ride was half an hour."

"You're magical," Ellie said holding her hands up to the side of her head. "You can read it in half a minute."

"But as you said, we don't have Martian DNA," Sam said pointing to her hand where DNA technically was.

"Fine," Ellie said turning around, annoyed at that pointless disagreement.

"If you hadn't been so busy fighting, you would know we have gotten to the fortress," Elizabeth said. Sam, Sofia, and the fairies walked out of the spaceship and on to Red Crystal Island.

"This is so weird," Sam said looking around the island with disgust. "It's so … red."

"Well it was made by Victoria," Sofia said looking around as she slipped her hand over her arm, because of the goosebumps she was getting from fear. "We have to keep going."

"Fine," Sam said tugging a little on braids she had made because she thought that her hair would be dysfunctional.

Sam started for the bridge onto the pool. "Why did they make this their fortress?"

"I kind of flooded it," Elizabeth said raising her hand like she was going to ask the teacher something. "They made me mad."

"Whatever," Sofia said. She joined Sam, and they stood before the contained pool. Ellie waved her hands, and Sam and Sofia disappeared and all they saw was red sand where their feet were.

"Where are they?" Elizabeth asked looking around the place. And then she squinted her eyes because of the liquid coming out of them. Then she wailed, "Did they ditch us?"

"Invisibility spell," Ellie said squinting her eyes too, but for a different reason. "Duh." Sam and Sofia flew toward the island where their Dad was trapped. They landed beside Dad, but he couldn't see them.

"Dad, it's me," Sofia whispered into his ear. "Invisibility spell."

"Sofia is that you?" Dad asked quietly looking at Victoria who was right before them.

"Yes, it's me. We're going to get you out of here," Sofia said. She reached for the knot in the rope, but as she did, pink magic drained from her hand, "It's a trap. The only way to get him out is to give up our magic."

"Why does she have to be so dang smart?" Sam asked.

As Sofia took her hand off the knot, Victoria stood up, she knew that her trap had just taken action. "You know you can let him go," Victoria paused like that was it, but Sam and Sofia knew the next horrible thing that was going to come out of her mouth. Or at least Sam thought it was horrible, "if you give up your magic."

The invisibility spell was lifted. "We can't let you harm this planet," Sofia said as she stood on a rock.

"I won't give it!" Sam shouted like her magic was a trillion dollars.

"Well, I can't only have Sofia's magic," Victoria said stomping her foot in anger on the Red Crystal Island. "I need both! Just do it."

Catalina raised her hands, and she vanished, along with Sam, Victoria, Dad, Elizabeth, and Ellie. But Sofia was left behind. She saw a small hint of a shadow in the distance. It started getting bigger, and bigger, and bigger, until it became a dragon.

Sofia tried a teleportation spell, but her powers weren't strong enough. "Come on," she complained trying again, and again. She couldn't get it to work.

Sam knew she should try to help, but she couldn't. It was the only way to save Dad. So she stood on Red Crystal Island, a few feet away from Sofia, for she had only teleported feet behind her. She felt like for every second, there was a day-long pause.

After a few seconds, Sofia finally got the teleportation to work, but she could only move to behind a rock, next to Sam, but she didn't notice her because she was too nervous. Luckily, the dragon couldn't see her. Sofia got ready to start flying.

"See? You can't have both your magic and your father," Victoria said too, because she was just a few feet behind Sam. "So now I will kill your father."

"No!" Sam shouted. "I love him, and Sofia. Can I keep both?"

"Okay," Victoria said suspiciously, "I'll give you a third option."

"Anything. I'll do anything," Sam pleaded.

"Your third option is ... join me."

"No," Sam said, "I can't. My sister would hate me even more." Suddenly, a bright pink light came into the corner of Sam's sight. It got closer.

Then a voice said, "I love you, Sam," and Sofia rushed through the air at what seemed like light speed. A million thoughts were going through her head. Will I survive? Will this help my father? Why didn't I notice Sam was here? Does she hate me?

But suddenly, Sofia stopped. "What?" she asked, confused looking around wondering why she randomly stopped.

"You think I didn't expect this?" Victoria said deviously. "I made a plan. If you accepted my offer, I'd have let you leave with your father and without your magic. But since this was expected, I put up a protection spell. And now I shall cast a spell. You and your Dad will forget Sam, and Sam will forget you two."

"But –" Sofia was cut off.

"No buts," Victoria said. "Now!"

Catalina randomly appeared in the crystals and moved her hands in a weird way, then the dragon, which was being a good dragon and hiding in the crystals, disappeared so he wouldn't be part of the sad conversation. Catalina then cast the spell of forgetfulness. White light spilled everywhere, and pictures of Sam showed up on the walls of crystals and in the air, then disappeared. Sam was no longer at their third birthday party. Sam wasn't at the recent funeral. And Sam saw the opposite for Dad and Sofia. They were forgetting everything. They had nothing to do with each other.

But Victoria let Sam and Sofia keep one memory. They remembered the moment they got magic. But that was it.

* * *

Later, Sofia walked to school with a frown on her face and that moment of magic hidden in her heart, like a dream. Something was missing. She wasn't even in the mood for cookie-dough ice cream. It was as though one day she had a happy life filled with everything she ever wanted, and now she felt like she was caught in a hole of emptiness.

CHAPTER 27:

SAM

Victoria watched as Sam stood with a clueless look on her face. Sam was in a cell of red wiring. And Victoria was in a spacecraft that had just taken off because she couldn't use the Red Crystal Island forever. Everything in this craft was see-through so you could see everything for however long is humanly possible. So cool. Victoria wondered what it felt like to have all her memories taken, from the beginning of her life until now, which is a twelve-year difference. She didn't feel a speck of empathy.

"Catalina, can you get her to use her powers?" Victoria asked as she stopped pacing repeatedly, waiting for Sam's powers to be used.

"Why?" Catalina wondered who was sitting there also waiting for her to use her powers, but less impatiently.

"I can't get her magic out of her until she uses it," Victoria said opening her eyes wider like she was going crazy.

Catalina walked into the holding room. But she didn't head for the red wire cell holding Sam. She went to the left, where there was a classic prison cell with poles and bars.

"What do you need?" Ellie asked sitting in a corner of the cell with tears smeared on her face, right next to Elizabeth, who literally had wet clothing from tears. She let her perfect, whitish-blonde hair down. Elizabeth glared at Catalina, who had just teleported into the cell.

"Get her to use her powers," Catalina said to the two sitting down in despair.

"You mean the clueless, pretty girl wandering around a cell with *a lot* of room?" Ellie asked looking over to where Sam was still wandering around her cell like a twelve-year-old who had lost all of her memories from an evil witch-like Martian.

"Just do it," Catalina said, raising her voice, and an echo sounded through the ship.

Ellie and Elizabeth were released from the cell and went straight toward Sam's cell because they knew if they didn't go directly, as Victoria said, they would be turned to a broom.

"Hey you! Use your magic!" Ellie said loudly pointing at Sam with a sharp finger.

"I think what Ellie means to say, is *please* use your magic," Catalina said, then turned toward Ellie with a tilted face of disappointment.

Sam looked at them with a tilted head too, for she was clueless to everything now.

"Oh, right. She doesn't speak English," Catalina said bringing her head to her face, "or any other language."

"We have to read her mind?" Elizabeth asked turning to Catalina with tears in her eyes, expecting the answer 'NO!'

"But we lost our powers," Ellie said interrupting the staring contest Catalina and Elizabeth were basically having.

"So?" Catalina asked. She looked at Elizabeth who now was sniffling using her shirt.

"By the way," Elizabeth said sniffling, and also wanting to change the subject as to not cry so much, "where is Sean?"

"He decided to leave because we were abandoning team members," Catalina said waving a hand as to shoo him away from their thoughts. "Coward."

Elizabeth and Ellie stood next to the cage. They made strange faces at Sam, but she looked bewildered.

Sam looked away, into the nothingness that surrounded her in the ship. Bright lights shown everywhere. She thought many curious thoughts that somewhat translated into this: *This is pretty. I see lots of purple, pink, blue, and all different colors.* She must feel lonely. Not knowing a single person. And then a single tear dropped out of Sam's eye. It fell, and as it touched the ground, fire started. Flames sparked everywhere.

Catalina walked across the see-through ground toward the two fairies. "How did you do that?" Catalina asked curiously.

"She felt sad," Elizabeth said blankly thinking of her personality, and what she was before the brainwash. "And she did it on her own."

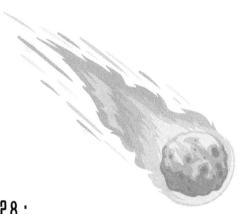

CHAPTER 28:

THE REMEMBRANCE

Sofia was walking home from school. She started out at a slow pace and watched the autumn leaves, which didn't fall because this is Florida. Oh how she missed Minnesota!

Sofia looked down at the sidewalk. She wondered why she was so excited when her life was so dull. She thought maybe, if she forced herself, she could at least have good memories.

Sofia still held onto the moment that she figured was a dream. She wondered what life would be like if that moment continued into real life.

Sofia felt like the sidewalk was an endless desert and she would never reach her home. Then her home appeared. But when she stepped inside, it didn't feel like home. Nowhere felt like home, ever since the day she realized how dull her life was.

She walked into the dining room and sat down in a chair. Sofia greeted her Dad, who sat on the other side of the dusty dinner table. Dinner was already set up, and she sipped her tomato soup.

"How was your day?" Dad asked sipping from his water which was in an 'I Love Dad' mug Sofia had gotten him earlier that year.

"Okay," Sofia responded scooping up some of her soup in a spoon, then letting it fall out, as small splashes gave her the slightest form of entertainment.

"Well, mine was great," Dad said straightening his back as he turned the other way probably to remember the day.

"Oh," Sofia said, unshocked by this news. "Why?"

"I met someone," Dad said looking at his hands, probably nervous.

"New best friend?" Sofia asked still looking at her soup in dismay.

"Well ..." Dad stared off into the kitchen with all the clean bowls and cups.

"You aren't dating are you?" Sofia asked, now looking up with attentive eyes.

"Her name is Mari."

"What are you thinking?" Sofia asked, raising her voice. "Is mom nobody anymore? Do you no longer love her? Are you crazy?!"

"It's just a thing," Dad said, with no defense.

"Oh! So, mom was just a thing?" Sofia yelled getting up from her seat.

"Well, you're going to have to get used to her, because she's going to be visiting a lot," Dad said also getting up from his seat, and he had his hand rested on the table.

A low, dark voice sounded from upstairs. "Have you told her yet?" Sofia heard footsteps go down the creaky stairs. The woman had black hair, green eyes, and super pale skin. "Hi. My name is Mari." The woman knelt to Sofia's height, but Sofia was tall so she ended up looking stupid, not like she didn't already.

Suddenly, so many memories flowed into Sofia. She had a twin named Sam. She had magic. She knew who Mari was. And she knew she had to take down that girlfriend-pretending, twin sister-stealing, death trap in the making, girl named Victoria.

CHAPTER 29:

A BUILDING RELATIONSHIP

Catalina and Victoria were watching American movies and musicals, cuddled up in their pajamas (whatever those are).

She had just gotten back from pretending to be Mari, the 'girlfriend' of Sofia's father.

"And your little dog, too!" Victoria said, referencing *The Wizard of Oz*. She looked over at Catalina. At first, Victoria had seen a stiff magical fairy doing whatever she was told. But now she saw a loose laughing friend who had personality and boldness, that Victoria knew meant good times were in their future of torturing Sam and Sofia. Friendship.

But Catalina couldn't be her friend. Business only.

Or maybe Victoria could be a bit friendly. No, she could not. What would happen if she accepted more than the magic business? Would it be so bad to have a laugh occasionally?

"How do you like the movie?" Catalina asked turning to Victoria who was under the covers, still intently focussed on the hologram of the movie placed in front of them.

"It's good," Victoria said now looking at Catalina who had a smile on her face. Then Victoria blinked a few times as she realized what they *should* be doing, "But we should start draining Sam's magic."

"I told you, we can't do that until we get Sofia. And you haven't been able to take her to your place," Catalina said who was probably making up excuses for the fact that she wanted to finish the movie.

"Well, there must be something you can do," Victoria said clearly trying to ignore the fact that she was becoming friendly.

"You could grab her in her sleep," Catalina said. She poofed into her hands some kernels of some type with yellowish stuff on them, that was presumably butter. She ate them hurriedly.

"And risk a surprise blast?" Victoria said, like she was absurd, still looking at the weird stuff in the bag.

"Then there's nothing we can do," Catalina said as she chewed a kernel.

"Did I just fight for your case?" Victoria said, laughing at herself.

"Yeah, you did," Catalina said, laughing a bit, too, now looking at Victoria.

They sat for a few more minutes and watched the movie. They wondered what to say next. Were they friends? Neither had the slightest idea.

When the movie ended, they walked through the cell area to get to their sleeping quarters. They laid in their separate beds to sleep. But they didn't sleep.

Victoria stared up at space and saw all the constellations. Victoria looked to the side and asked Catalina, "Do you want to look at the stars?"

"Sure." Catalina used her magic to put the beds closer together.

"I see a pony," Victoria said, pointing to the constellation with a beautiful starry mane.

"I see something that looks like a dipper," Catalina said now looking all the way to the other side of the skylight.

"I see a maybe new friend?" Victoria asked shutting her eyes tightly as she turned a little from Catalina. After all she was very frightened. Had she ruined everything? Or would Catalina not mind? She for sure was clueless.

"I see one, too," Catalina said, about to hug Victoria. But they didn't because it would be awkward. So they just waited until they drifted off to sleep, thinking about the fun night they had.

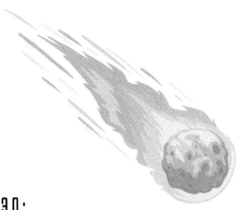

CHAPTER 30:

ATTACK!

Sofia knew she had to get her sister back from the – wherever. But she had no idea where the "wherever" was located.

She flew throughout the galaxy for a few thousand miles, but she saw nothing from Earth. But then she remembered Mari—or Victoria. Victoria would have to take Sam to the station, and she would be there. But she would have her captured. Or would she expect Sofia would come and escape free? It was a risk. But Sofia was willing to take any risk for her sister.

Sofia ran down the stairs to the dining room. 'Mari' was at the table. "Why doesn't Dad ever go to your place?" Sofia asked as she caught her breath.

"Well, I never thought about it," Mari said with a pretend high-pitched noise hiding the fact of her evil existence. "Do you want to come over and check the place out?" Mari said as she looked at her with an evil glint in her eyes, that only the witch Victoria could have.

"I guess so," Sofia said dazing off into the sky trying not to make eye contact with 'Mari.' If she did Victoria might know

Sofia knows everything. She had to be realistic, so she added, "But shouldn't my dad be over there first?"

"Well, I want you to check it out to see if ... if it's good enough."

"Okay," Sofia said, wondering what 'Mari' meant by that. "When?"

"How about right now?" Mari suggested bringing out probably fake keys that led to no door in the universe. "You don't mind. Right, sweetie?"

"Of course not," Dad said, totally cool with the idea his little girl was going to go into a random strangers' house, which might not even be a house. "I want my daughter and my girlfriend to have a relationship, right?"

"Good," Mari said jumping just a tad bit, "let's go."

They walked out of the door. And I can tell you they didn't walk back in.

* * *

"This way," Mari said, pointing toward the left, then right.

"What street is your home on?" Sofia teased 'Mari'.

"Z Street?" Mari said nodding after waiting about three seconds.

"That street is over two miles away," Sofia said knowing that Z Street was not a street.

"Miles?" Mari asked tilting her head still going straight.

Sofia knew that Mari would realize that Sofia knew she was Victoria unless she did something to cover it up. "Are you from a different country? Because most countries use the metric system, and the metric system doesn't apply here."

"Yes," Victoria said nodding still looking straight with a confused look.

Bang, bang, bang!

"Sorry, but I have to call this person," Victoria said as she walked to the left side of the sidewalk. "I got her," Victoria whispered, and she took a picture of Sofia, who knew she was being watched.

"Good," the voice which was probably Catalina said.

"Ready to teleport."

Suddenly a green light beamed down on top of Sofia. But before it teleported her to the spaceship, a figure appeared and jumped at her.

"Why did you do that?" asked Sofia. She reached up and touched a new scratch on the left side of her face. "Sean? What are you doing here?" Suddenly Sean made a blast out of his hands toward Victoria, and she stood still frozen. She was about to grab Sofia.

"I'm trying to keep you safe," Sean said turning his head toward Sofia. She noticed that he was wearing camouflage and was probably watching her because he knew the dangers of Victoria, and that he can help a little bit. "And you're not helping."

"I was going to get my sister back," Sofia said pointing to the green beam which she clearly wanted to jump into.

"Then I'm coming with you," Sean said, with no doubt in his voice.

"Why?" Sofia asked still staying in the position she was in when Victoria was frozen. "You must have a great life. No ruler, alone, with magic."

"But I want to help you," Sean said as he made a spell to heal Sofia's cut.

"Why?" Sofia exclaimed loudly. She then looked around hoping no one was seeing this scene.

"'Cause ... because I — Victoria said she was going to take over Earth. And you would die. And your father, and Sam, and her whole crew. Including me."

"I'm sorry, but I have to do this," Sofia said looking at Sean with new tears in her eyes. "But you can come."

"Kay," Sean said as he lifted the spell that had frozen Victoria. She flinched then stood calmly.

"Do you two know each other?" Mari asked probably thinking Sofia still had no memories.

"He goes to my school," Sofia said quickly. "He started this week."

"Okay," Mari said breathing deeply avoiding having an annoyed look, that had already appeared on her face. "I'll be right back." Mari walked away and talked to Catalina again.

"Hold my hand," Sean said.

"Eww," Sofia said. "Why?"

"We're going to the ship now," Sean whispered as he grabbed her hand which was warm from the cement ground.

"Okay," Sofia said shutting her eyes tightly.

"Here we go."

* * *

Sofia and Sean landed on the station ready for battle. "Attack!" shouted Sofia. She flew through the air incredibly fast, until she reached Sam's cell.

When she saw her sister, Sam's memories flowed back in colors. Light. Fun. Magic. Happiness. "Sofia?" Sam asked through the red wire.

"We're going to get you out of there," Sofia promised. She zoomed through the room again to get to Sean.

"Let's get your sister back," Sean announced getting in a ready position for attack.

Sofia looked at Catalina and Victoria, who were storming toward them, "We'll see about that."

CHAPTER 31:

THE BATTLE

Sam tried with all her magic to get out of the red wire cage, but nothing seemed to work.

"Come on!" Sam exclaimed. She couldn't get out, so she started thinking. She remembered what had happened last night. Victoria refused to tell Sam who she was, and then Catalina personally took her to the cage. *They must be friends now. Well evil will like evil.*

Sam wondered when the battle would be over and when she could go back home and have hot cocoa with their Dad, even though it was still early fall. She wondered when things would be normal.

* * *

Sofia ran straight for Victoria. She put out her hand, created a cotton candy ball, and threw it at Victoria's face. "What?" Sofia asked when Sean looked at her strangely. "Just because we are battling doesn't mean I can't have personality." Next, Sofia threw a blast that looked like a cat. It hit Victoria in the face again and started biting. It took her to the ground... for a few seconds. But as Sofia threw each blast she hoped that her morality wasn't fading. She didn't want to be as ruthlessly evil as Victoria. She wanted to be careful not to kill her.

"Give me my sister," Sofia said. She placed her foot on Victoria's chest, but didn't put weight on it because that could kill her.

Victoria had fear in her eyes as she stared up at Sofia panting. Then Catalina came storming behind.

"She will never." Catalina tossed Sofia across the room, and she hit the wall. Her spine felt broken, like she would never heal from the hard hit.

Sofia used her magic to immediately mend herself, turned herself invisible, and walked over to Catalina. Sofia found the key to the cage and snatched it away from the stand it was on when Sean and Sofia invaded. Catalina was running after her but Sean did a spell to make her go in a loop, so Catalina was immediately on the other side of the glass ship, which by the way was a marvelous use of magic glass.

"What?" asked Catalina as she kept running, suddenly realizing she was behind where she was before. It was confusing on the ship. It looked like you were standing on nothing, even though there was glass and auto-gravity.

Sofia got to the cage and let Sam free. "Thank you," Sam said as she quickly ran out the door.

"Hey, will you free us, too?" Elizabeth asked tears with all over her face from being rejected.

Just as Sean was looking over at Sofia, and Sofia was looking at Ellie and Elizabeth, and Ellie and Elizabeth were looking at Sofia, and Sam was looking at Victoria, Victoria and Catalina assumed that no one was looking at them and ran to hide behind a fallen over desk from one of Sofia's spells. Sam didn't dare go over.

"Coming." Sofia flew down to the cell. "Go fight, Sam." Sam flew off to go about fifty feet away from the table Catalina and Victoria were behind, and Sofia unlocked the cell.

"Thanks," Ellie said. The fairies checked their magic. Ellie sent off pixie dust randomly which blinded them with a bright light for thirty seconds, and then Elizabeth sent out a small wave of magic that was supposed to flood the ears with a noise that would make them not hear for about a strong thirty seconds.

"We've got to fight," Sofia said holding a fist which had magical curves and lights around it showing a weird smell was coming.

"Let's go," Elizabeth said as she faced Sam who she knew was getting ready for battle against the worst (but only) villain they knew.

* * *

"We need to win," Victoria said as she ducked from one of Sofia's crazy spells that sent out sharpened paper, and when you get hit, you wouldn't move for roughly a minute. Catalina learned that the hard way.

"I have not gone this far just to fail," Catalina replied as she sent out a spell too which caused them to be trapped in ice cream at the shoulders for thirty seconds. Brutal, but delicious.

"Let's get out there," Victoria said. She changed from Mari's clothes, which were a dark green dress with itchy long sleeves, to a nice black dress, sleeveless at that, with a black leather jacket that was unzipped and hanging from her shoulders, along with shockingly high heels that made her almost a foot taller, all with the swish of a finger.

Catalina stepped out and made a wave of chainsaws intended to kill. Everyone dodged them except Sean.

"Oww!" Sean fell to the floor. The cut in his hand went deep. Sofia waved her hand over it to mend it, but it did nothing. She tried again, still nothing. Sofia looked at Catalina in deep confusion. The question her face was, *why?* "Cast!" Sofia created a cast around the arm. "Get better."

"Only I can heal it instantly, you know," Catalina said as she squinted her eyes like Sofia was stupid, which was not a fact.

Sofia created a wave, an actual wave.

Water surrounded Catalina, but eventually she broke out. She went over to Victoria. "Have you been helping at all?" Catalina asked, with wide eyes of annoyance, as she magically dried herself. "This is your battle."

"You have stronger powers," Victoria said. She looked at her nails.

"Fine," Catalina said as she quickly pulled her hands toward her and then forcefully pushed them together, with a bucketload of anger, "but you're helping me come up with a plan."

"Okay." Victoria looked bored.

"We need to give them something they want in exchange for their magic. Or we should tell them the benefits of combining our magic, like making a person love you, or bringing back the dead or—" Catalina was cut off.

"Wait," Victoria said. Then terribly, with no mercy or consent for anyone's emotions she said, "I have an idea."

CHAPTER 32:

PUNISHMENT OF NO DEAL

Sam, Sofia, and their team members all blasted Victoria and Catalina with a spell they agreed on: Candy Blast.

"Think of flying," Ellie said, and she used her magic pixie dust to flip them in the air.

"Think devastating thoughts," Elizabeth whispered, and she sent of a wave of sorrow and fear, along with a few hammers and screwdrivers, to puncture Catalina and Victoria. For a second, they looked depressed.

"Everybody stop!" Victoria said loudly as she held up her hands. "We have a message for Sam and Sofia. We were going to combine our powers with yours to have a ton of magic, so," Victoria paused as she showed a blue bag that looked like a backpack. "This is meant for turning magic into a substance that can be absorbed by living creatures. With our new powers, one of the many things we could do is bring back the dead."

Sofia and Sam knew where this was going and knew this would be a hard decision.

"If Sam and Sofia willingly give us their powers, we will bring back their Mom. Do you accept?" Victoria looked around the room.

Sam and Sofia thought over the opportunity. They thought about how much it would cost the Martians. They looked at each other. Each saw the fear in the other's eyes. Sofia was thinking about how she secretly had dreams of Mom at night, and that it would be nice to see her. Sam thought about how much she loved Mom, and what her life could be with her around. It was a tough choice, and whichever answer they chose, they would regret.

Sam spoke first. She raised her hand. "I will do it."

Sofia looked at Sam like she had said she was about to eat a car. "That's so selfish. Sam, imagine if you were a Martian who would have to be ruled by this tyrant."

"But it will get Mom back," Sam said with a tear of loss in her eye, just wanting to burst out.

"Fine," Sofia said, realizing she too had a tear in her eye. "Do what you want. Just know that your decision could cost others their lives."

"Well, you have to accept too," Victoria said loudly as her eyes rolled, "or else there won't be enough magic."

"I'll give my sister a bit of time to see the priority here," Sam said chuckling a little bit nervously. "Remember, *I* accept." She put out her hand. Victoria shook it and, as she did, Sam grabbed her arm and pushed her to a window on the other side of the room.

"Open!" Sam shouted, hoping Sofia caught the cue.

Sofia took her hands, grabbed some air, and trapped it in her hand. Suddenly, almost everything stopped. Nothing moved but Sofia, Sam, and a struggling Victoria. Sofia opened her palm and raised it. As she raised her hand, the window opened. Sofia simultaneously cast another spell, and Sam breathed in deeply, for now she had oxygen. Victoria also had carbon dioxide. Suddenly Sam felt a little warmness. She realized space is cold, so of course she had to cast a spell for heat. Thank god for her intelligence!

"Why did you come after us?" Sam asked as she held Victoria in the air.

"Power," Victoria said. She sounded as if she didn't have one regret.

"Okay," Sofia said nodding. "If that is so, and if you're going to release your wrath on Mars, I guess this is worth it."

"Don't do it," Sam said knowing clearly what was going to happen.

Sofia flew into the air. "I have to," Sofia said. She used her magic to glue Sam and the rest of the people to the ground, including Catalina. All stared at her with curious eyes. Sofia cast a spell that froze everyone, except for Sofia and Victoria.

I've killed before. Everyone's eyes went toward Sofia as she tried to do a spell to destroy Victoria. Sofia couldn't hear them, because their oxygen wasn't connected, and they didn't have a magical connection. She made a pulling motion, but it made her float toward Victoria. Then a great sucking force pulled Sofia and Victoria to the edge of the window.

Sofia looked over at Victoria, who was suffering with no carbon dioxide. Sofia willed her arm to create a bubble of carbon dioxide and gave it to Victoria. Then the sucking was so strong that Victoria let go. Sofia looked to Sam, distress in her eyes, as Sofia started to let go, and made Victoria teleport. Sofia put her on a random planet that she would do a spell to find the name of. But that was off topic. She let go.

Sam focused her hand toward Sofia and tried with all her might to pull her back inside. Slowly, Sofia floated toward the open window in the space station. As she went through the hole, Sam took her other arm and made the window like new. Sam gave oxygen to the whole room, and everyone looked at Sofia, who was lying on the floor.

Sam started to cry, but Elizabeth took her hand and healed Sofia. When Sofia came to life, she stood slowly and looked at Sam, who was leaning over with wiped tears all over her face.

"You did it!" Sofia said as she ran over and hugged her. "Where is Victoria now?"

"She's on..." Sam paused because the name she heard was hard to pronounce. "Durstine?"

"So it's over, and all that's left of her is this flash drive," Sofia said as she picked it up. She hadn't noticed this before, but she just wanted to point it out.

"What do you think is on it?" Sam asked as she grabbed it from Sofia's hand.

"I don't know. Let's check it out." Sofia grabbed the flash drive back and put it into a computer she created with magic. A video link showed up. She pressed "play" on the video.

"Hello, Sam and Sofia," Victoria said on the recording. "If you are watching this, it means my plans failed. So, the point of this video is to say I probably will feel like I want to have a last taste of revenge. So right now, this is what's happening." A corner of the screen showed what the street cameras saw, that always looked at their house. A flame showed just a glint out of a window. Dust came off the house and fell onto their garden. Everything in their childhood was now gone because of a simple flash drive. Or was it because of some magic? Which came first didn't matter.

Anger filled the twins. It felt like suddenly a flame was lit in their heart, and the only emotions they could feel was the anger that the fire made them experience. But then the fire in their heart just froze somehow. The ice was lonely cold in their hearts. Immense sadness. And the fire only grew, like their anger and sadness, until it covered the whole house, or heart.

"I hope you enjoy being orphans!" Victoria said, as she just expected that there would be silence for a few seconds. She gave an evil laugh. "Mwahaha. Oh, and Sofia? Remember that feeling after you used that magic? That was me," Victoria said with a wink.

"No!" Sofia and Sam both screamed at the same time, then looked down at their shoes. The rest of the video showed more recordings of the house burning. It was a long reminder of how their life might as well have been burned down. So many memories took place there. This was where they shared stories about their first crushes, ended up hating them by the way. It was where Dad told them how he and Mom met at a college party, when they both tripped and fell in the pool. Mom's first words to Dad were "What an idiot." The last time they saw their Mom; she said, "I'll be right back after I get back from Italy," Mom had said, "I love you," then she walked out of the door for the last time.

And now another parent gone. He had taught them how to tie their shoes. He had tried to help with the homework, however Mom really was who had thrusted them ahead of the average. And most of all he had provided, loved, cared, but really, he did most everything for the twins after Mom died. What Victoria had said about being orphans, was true.

"I thought she had reasons for trying to kill us, but she is heartless," Sofia cried sniffling. Shock caught up with her. Multiple tears swished down her cheeks. "Not that it was a good reason anyway!"

"We need to take something of Victoria's," Sam said, holding back her own tears. "Something important."

"No," Sofia said looking at Sam who was now much taller than Sofia because she had fallen on the ground. "We can't. If we do, we will become like Victoria."

"Fine," Sam said wiping her tears which finally overcame the barriers of her eyelids. "Then what can we do?"

"Mourn," Sofia answered. She looked down again.

The video kept playing.

"She took our father," Sam argued red in the face.

"We can't be her," Sofia retaliated, snot and tears wiped all over her face. Sadness would be their leading emotion. If they hadn't said which emotion they had, each would assume sadness.

"Oh my gosh!" They turned toward the video. "No!" a figure screamed as it ran toward where the burning house. The figure dropped a bag of groceries. "What happened?!"

The video zoomed in and showed that the figure had stress wrinkles, brown hair, and blue eyes. It was Dad!

"Dad!" Sofia screamed. It was like her whole life she had a fifty-pound weight on her back, and finally she could take it off. Like tears the size of the world were coming out her eyes.

"Oh my gosh, it's Dad!" Sam screamed, too, as she turned to the video, with smeared tears, the same feeling as Sofia. They both looked to the other fairies, who were strapped down and silent because they didn't want to interrupt this moment of mixed emotions.

"We have to go," Sofia said turning to Sam like it was obvious, which it was.

"We'll see you later, guys," Sam said. She turned away, creating a portal hurriedly.

"We're coming with you," Elizabeth responded before Sam had the chance to jump in.

"We are?" Ellie asked who clearly wasn't paying the most attention to the whole situation.

Elizabeth gave her a look of sadness, as she realized she wouldn't agree with her. Tears flooded down.

"I mean, we are," said Ellie nodding, looking to Elizabeth with regret in her eyes.

"Okay," Sofia said with a smile still on her face. "Let's go." She waved her fingers, and everyone in the room teleported. They stood on the sidewalk and watched the fire. A spell was cast so Catalina was captured in magical handcuffs and couldn't move.

"Hey!" Catalina screamed finally. "Victoria won't stand for this."

"Blah, blah, whatever," Sam said waving a hand. Then waved a hand at Dad and his memories of her came back. Not those of Red Crystal Island. Too painful. She looked back at Catalina, "We'll deal with you later."

"Girls!" Dad jogged over to them. Then looked curiously at the crowd with a lot of scrapes, now realizing how they got hurt. But just a bit. "Do you know what happened? And who are these people?"

"Dad," Sofia said, changing the subject, "we have something to tell you."

"What is it?" Dad asked with a smile on his face as he brought a hand to her shoulder. The warmth of his hand felt so rare, from the near-death experience. But she would never tell him of what she saw.

"We have magic."

CHAPTER 33:

CATHERINE

Catalina sat on a chair Sam and Sofia created for her.

"Did Victoria put a spell on you?" Sofia asked Catalina as she began to sit on the couch they made.

Sam thought it was a beautiful autumn day in the park, while people were looking at them strangely for creating a chair. But at least it was a change from that strange spaceship made of glass, they were basically imprisoned on.

"Well, of course she did," Catalina answered cutting Sam out of her thoughts.

"What did it exactly do?" Sam asked as she shook her head almost unnoticably.

"It made me a person who would follow Victoria's orders," Catalina answered shaking her head. It felt like her next sentence would only consist of 'duh,' but she closed her mouth. Sam assumed it was out of fear, so she felt a little honored, and a little sorry.

"Did it make you a new person overall?" Sofia asked looking at Catalina, trying not to pay attention to the people all staring at them.

"What's with the questions?" Catalina asked probably trying to dodge the question.

"We are the ones asking the questions. Now, answer," Sam said trying to make it look like she hadn't been dozing the whole conversation.

"It did," Catalina blurted with annoyance in her voice.

"Can we reverse it?" Sofia asked making weird hand movements.

"Why are you asking these questions?" Catalina asked as she started to intently stare at Sam and Sofia's eyes with despair, and annoyance.

"We want to see if we can make you a good person instead of locking you up," Sofia answered tilting her head a bit. "I think I said that right."

"I thought it was so we could play a *really* good game of interrogation," Sam said to Sofia with a glint of humor in her dazzling (and no longer dozing) eyes.

Catalina gave them a glance, clearly not understanding the concept of a joke.

"Well it might be, depending on the next answer," Sofia said in her defense. "Can we reverse the spell?"

"You can," Catalina admitted in a slouching position now, "but I will never tell you how."

"Excuse my partner and I as we discuss," Sam said as she led Sofia a few feet away off the couch. "Shouldn't we make a reverse spell that works on everything?"

"Well, our powers can create powers, can't they?" Sofia asked tilting her head far too much. "Ow."

"Let's go," Sam said, knowing their answer and walking back to Catalina.

"Reverse!" Sam and Sofia pointed their hands at Catalina, and her eyes turned black. Catalina was shaking while flying in the air in the chair. She screamed something so high-pitched, it made her own ears bleed. The darkness in her eyes dripped out, revealing her eyes were now brown. Once all the darkness had left, the screaming stopped and ebbed away into nothing. Catalina floated down to the ground.

She now had blonde hair, brown eyes, and was wearing a T-shirt that says 'People say it's raining cats and dogs. I go outside and come in with nothing.' She turned around, and it said in bold letters, standing out against the faded red, 'DISAPPOINTMENT.'

"Catalina?" Sam asked as she blinked many times to adjust her sight.

"Are you okay?" Sofia asked walking up with squinted eyes too.

Catalina's eyes came into focus, and she said, "Who's Catalina? My name is Catherine."

"Okay, *Catherine,*" Sam corrected as her eyes were returning to normal. "What is the last thing you remember?"

"I was on my way to Advanced Animal Magic Class." Catherine said holding her fingers out trying to remember something. "Then I fell to the ground, and I couldn't see anything. I woke up in a large dark cell and was there for a *very* long time. I went out again, and then I ended up here a few seconds later," Catherine finished.

"Well, what happened is, this Martian named Victoria took over your body, and you must've become a new person somehow," Sofia said as she looked around her to make sure she was real.

"Oh," Catherine said as she brought up her hands for a quick second. "The Curse That Steals Your Body. The fairy comminitee hasn't come up with the best names..."

"Well, you can go carry on with your life," Sam said shooing her away as she turned around. "'Bye."

"You saved me, didn't you?" Catherine asked, bringing her hand to her sports shorts with a few blue stripes on them.

"Yes, we did," Sofia said, proud of herself, as she stood a little taller.

"Then I owe you," Catherine insisted.

"You don't need to," Sofia said with an endearing look as she put her hair around her ears.

"But it also sounds fun," Catherine said dancing just a bit.

"Almost dying to save a whole planet?" Sam asked like she was crazy.

"I insist," Catherine replied as she nodded quickly.

"Fine," Sam said with a smile on her face, feeling like *I inspired someone to as she calls it 'owe me.'* "If you really want to."

"What should I do for now?" Catherine asked with a satisfied change in her voice.

"Just hang around, until we need you," Sam answered shrugging her shoulders a bit.

"Okay," Catherine said nodding, and smiling. "See you later."

CHAPTER 34:

ELEANOR

Sam and Sofia walked to the field near the park, where they were camping with Dad until they got a new home.

"Catalina ended up being a different person," Sam said, starting an idea.

"Yeah?" Sofia asked as she looked up from her hands, still slouching, however.

"Well, what do you think about Elizabeth and Ellie?" Sam asked fully focussed on Sofia. "Oh, also Sean, but it seems he was nice, just... not part of the spell."

"Maybe," Sofia answered a bit skeptical.

"Should we check?" Sam asked getting up from the chair ready to walk over where the group was sitting.

"Does that need to be a question?" Sofia asked as she walked through the field to the bench they were at. It was a cloudy day, but at least they had nothing to worry about... yet.

* * *

"So, all you have to do is sit still," Sofia said as she made a hand motion for them to come by where Sam and Sofia were sitting. Ellie and Elizabeth sat in plastic chairs at the campsite.

"Wait. Why?" Elizabeth asked quickly, "Are you trying to kill me? I thought we were friends."

"We are not going to kill you!" Sam said annoyed from the repetitive sensitiveness. "I hope she changes."

"Let's get on with it," Sofia said agreeing, but not wanting to say so.

"Reverse!" Sam and Sofia both shouted like last time.

Elizabeth's eyes turned white and she rose into the air, but Ellie and Sean still sat normally.

"Why aren't you like creepy girl over there?" Sam asked not paying attention to the light Elizabeth was creating for a reason.

"I guess I was never a different person," Ellie said. She walked out of her seat trying to avoid the light and the people who kept looking at the glowing fairy.

Elizabeth came down after Ellie left, but Sean sat silently.

"What happened, Elizabeth?" Sofia asked as she blinked a few times.

"Who's Elizabeth?" Elizabeth asked squinting her eyes a bit, "I'm Eleanor."

"Wait. Test," Sam said holding her hands in front of Sofia. "Someone got rid of you. Why do you think they did it?"

"Because they didn't realize how great moi is!" Eleanor responded in a higher and enthusiastic voice.

The twins looked at each other with happiness. Sofia said, "Looks like we have a new team member."

Finally, Sean broke out of silence, "Three! I'll make sure Ellie is part of this. Not being evil by the way!"

CHAPTER 35:

BYE BYE, BULLY

Sam and Sofia flew to school. It was the first day since they got back from battling Victoria.

"I can't believe I'm saying this, but I'm excited to be back to normal life," Sam said as she flew past the last block toward school. They landed safely, outside of the door.

"Here we go," Sofia said, now confident.

"Here we go," Sam repeated.

* * *

Max the Meanie was picking on kids for getting a high grade.

"If you get an A + in anything it would be weirdness!" He said getting all up in their faces. He stood back wearing his quote-unquote 'iconic' leather jacket.

"Stop being so mean!" Sofia interrupted as she jogged over to the scene.

"Yeah," Sam agreed as she got closer too. "Being smart isn't bad or annoying. It's helpful for the future, and you will regret being so mean to them!"

"Fine," Max said as he backed away with his hands up toward his friends. He turn around and ran.

And just to say the school petitioned a no bullying rule that would have strict constraints, and of course Max didn't follow it so he was expelled. Again just to say. Back to fifth grade…

CHAPTER 36:

THERE WILL BE NO END

Sam and Sofia walked around the campsite in the, unusual for Sam and Sofia, humid autumn air. They were celebrating with a party for Victoria's defeat.

Everyone gathered around the magic-made fire and started smoking their hot dogs.

"Hello, people," Sofia projected. Everyone stared at her.

"During this journey, we have gone through many challenges," Sam said hesitantly and gulped.

"All have been hard to accomplish and hard to get out of. Everything about it was hard," Sofia said putting her hands up in a petty, but cute way.

"But after all the things that have happened, many good things have happened, too." Sam looked at Ellie, Sean, Sofia, Catherine, and Eleanor. "Magic, experience, confidence, and new companions."

"And after all this, we have also learned that if you fight as hard as you can for your goal and stay true to yourself and who you are becoming, you will always win," Sofia said turning around to her father who had a face of true pride.

"So even though we have magic and have defeated Victoria, our challenges are far from over," Sam said nodding toward Sofia. "College, bullies [solved not so far in the future], money, it's endless."

"So we need to be grateful for the moments in-between like tonight, but know, that this is not the end," Sofia said holding up her magic made glass of water like it was approaching an end.

"There never will be an end. Not one," Sam finished. Sam sat down with everyone else.

"Also, Sofia? What was Victoria talking about when she said you felt guilty or something?"

"I kind of ... I killed two people, and I think that's how she tracked us down."

"What?" Sam looked down in doubt and wonder. "You know what? It's okay. We've all been under pressure, and I'm sure you have a good reason." Sam and Sofia hugged. Then Sam looked down again in deep wonder, as she thought of her sister's mistake. Did Sofia do it for a good cause?

"They were Martians working for a reward who wanted to kill us," Sofia whispered as she stayed in a hug.

Sam's question was answered.

The twins thought they would not encounter Victoria again. But as they said, there would be no end. Not now, not ever.

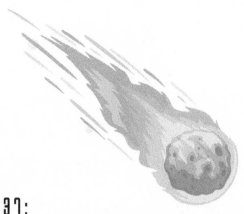

CHAPTER 37:

I'M COMING

"No!" Victoria screamed.

Victoria watched a video. She saw Dad surviving, Sofia falling into a happy life, Sam becoming an enthusiastic survivor, and her best friend, Catalina, dissolving into nothing.

Victoria knew she had to come up with a plan to get Sam and Sofia back. They had taken her best friend, her magic, and her future. Her heart was smashed with a hammer, and when it showed a sliver of life, the lungs failed [all an expression by the way].

After she picked up her backpack, she took out the magical orb she saved from the palace on Mars. She placed her hand on the top, and white beams surged through her body. Soon, they turned green.

"Now I have full-powered magic, and I am going to take advantage of it. I'm coming for you, Sam and Sofia."